The Early Stories
of Truman Capote

Foreword by Hilton Als

PENGUIN BOOKS

PENGUIN CLASSICS

UK | USA | Canada | Ireland | Australia
India | New Zealand | South Africa

Penguin Books is part of the Penguin Random House group of companies
whose addresses can be found at global.penguinrandomhouse.com.

First published in the United States of America by Random House,
an imprint and division of Random House LLC, a Penguin Random House Company 2015
First published in Great Britain in Penguin Classics 2015

001

The following stories were originally published in *The Green Witch*: "Parting of the
Way" (January 1940); "Swamp Terror" (June 1940); "The Moth in the Flame"
(December 1940); "Miss Belle Rankin" (December 1941); "Hilda," "Louise," and
"Lucy" (all May 1941).
The following stories appeared in German in *Zeit* in 2013: "Swamp Terror," "Miss
Belle Rankin," and "This Is for Jamie."

Printed in Great Britain by Clays Ltd, St Ives plc

A CIP catalogue record for this book is available from the British Library

ISBN: 978-0-241-20240-1

www.greenpenguin.co.uk

Foreword
by Hilton Als

Truman Capote stands in the middle of his motel room watching the TV. The motel is in the middle of the country—Kansas. It's 1963. The crummy carpet beneath his feet is stiff but it's the stiffness that helps hold him up—especially if he's had too much to drink. Outside, the western wind blows and Truman Capote, a glass of scotch in hand, watches the TV. It's one way he gets to relax after a long day in Garden City or its environs as he researches and writes *In Cold Blood*, his nonfiction novel about a multiple murder and its consequences. Capote began the book in 1959, but at first it wasn't a book; it was a magazine article for *The New Yorker*. As originally conceived by the author, the piece was meant to describe a small community and its response to a killing. But by the time he arrived in Garden City—the murders had been committed in nearby Holcomb—Perry Smith and Richard Hickock had been arrested and charged with slaying farm owners Mr. and Mrs. Herbert Klutter and their young children, Nancy and Kenyon; as a consequence of that arrest, Capote's project shifted focus, got more involved. On this particular late afternoon, though, *In Cold Blood* was about two years away from being finished. It's 1963, and Truman Capote stands in front of the TV. He's almost forty and he's been a writer for nearly as long as he's been alive. Words, stories, tales—he's been at it since he was a child, growing up in Louisiana and rural Alabama and then Connecticut and New York—a citizen formed by a divided world and opposing cultures: in his native South there was segregation, and, up north, at least talk of assimilation. In both places there was his intractable queerness. And the queerness of being a writer. "I started writing when I was eight," Capote said, once. "Out of the blue, uninspired by any example. I'd never known anyone who wrote; indeed, I knew few people who read." Writing, then, was his, just as his gayness—or, more specifically, his observant, critical, amused homosexual sensibility— was his, too. One would serve the other. "The most interesting writing I did during those days," Capote wrote of his wunderkind years, "was the plain everyday observations that I recorded in my journal. Descriptions of a neighbor. . . . Local gossip. A kind of reporting, a style of 'seeing' and 'hearing' that would later seriously influence me, though I was unaware of it then, for all my 'formal' writing, the stuff that I published and carefully typed, was more or less fictional." And yet it is the reportorial voice in Capote's early short stories, here collected for the first time, that remains among the work's more poignant features—along with his careful depiction of difference. From "Miss Belle Rankin," a story about misfits in a small southern town, written when Capote was seventeen:

> I was eight the first time I saw Miss Belle Rankin. It was a hot August day. The sun was waning in the scarlet-streaked sky, and the heat was rising dry and vibrant from the earth.
>
> I sat on the steps of the front porch, watching an approaching negress, and wondered how she could ever carry such a huge bundle of laundry on top of her head. She stopped and in reply to my greeting, laughed, that dark, drawling negro laughter. It was then that Miss Belle came walking slowly down the opposite side of the street. . . .

I saw her many times afterwards, but that first vision, almost like a dream, will always remain the clearest—Miss Belle, walking soundlessly down the street, little clouds of red dust rising about her feet as she disappeared into the dusk.

We will return to that Negress and Capote's relationship to blackness throughout the early part of his career in a moment. For now, let's treat this Negress as a real figment of the author's time and place of origin, a kind of painful literary artifact or black "shadow," as Toni Morrison has it, who took many forms in novels by white Depression-era heavy hitters such as Hemingway and Faulkner and Capote's much-admired Willa Cather. When she appears in "Miss Belle Rankin," Capote's clearly different narrator distances himself from her by calling attention to her "drawling negro laughter," and being easily spooked: at least whiteness saves him from *that*. 1941's "Lucy" is told from another young male protagonist's point of view. This time, though, he's looking to identify with a black woman who's treated as property. Capote writes: "Lucy was really the outgrowth of my mother's love for southern cooking. I was spending the summer in the south when my mother wrote my aunt and asked her to find her a colored woman who could really cook and would be willing to come to New York. After canvassing the territory, Lucy was the result." Lucy is lively, and loves show business as much as her young white companion does. As a matter of fact, she loves to imitate those singers—Ethel Waters among them—who delights them both. But is Lucy—and maybe Ethel?—performing a kind of female Negro behavior that's delightful because it's familiar? Lucy is never herself because Capote does not give her a self. Still, there is yearning for some kind of character, a soul and body to go along with what the young writer is really examining, which also happens to be one of his great themes: outsiderness. More than Lucy's race there is her southerness in a cold climate—a climate that the narrator, clearly a lonely boy the way Capote, the only child of an alcoholic mother, was a lonely boy, identifies with. Still, Lucy's creator cannot make her real because his own feelings of difference are not real to himself—he wants to get a handle on them. (In his 1979 story Capote writes of his 1932 self: "I had a secret, something that was bothering me, something that was really worrying me very much, something I was afraid to tell anybody, *any*body—I couldn't imagine what their reaction would be, it was such an odd thing that was worrying me, that had been worrying me for almost two years." Capote wanted to be a girl. And after he confesses it to someone he thinks might help him achieve that goal, she laughs.) In "Lucy" and elsewhere, sentiment caulks his sharp, original vision; Lucy belongs to Capote's desire to belong to a community, both literary and actual: when he wrote the piece he could not give up the white world just yet; he could not forsake the majority for the isolation that comes with being an artist. "Traffic West" was a step in the right direction or a preview of his mature style. Composed of a series of short scenes, the piece is a kind of mystery story about faith and the law. It begins:

> Four chairs and a table. On the table, paper—in the chairs, men. Windows above the street. On the street, people—against the window, rain. This was, perhaps, an abstraction, a painted picture only, but the people, innocent, unsuspecting, moved below, and the the rain fell wet on the window. For the men stirred not, the legal, precise document, on the table moved not.

Capote's cinematic eye—the movies influenced him as much as books and conversation did—was sharpened as he produced these apprentice works, and their value, essentially, is watching where pieces like "Traffic West" led him, technically speaking. Certainly that story was the apprentice work he needed to write to get to "Miriam," an amazing tale about a disenfranchised older woman living in an alienating New York covered in snow. (Capote published "Miriam" when he was just twenty.) And, of course, stories like "Miriam" led to other cinema-inspired narratives like 1950's "A Diamond Guitar," which, in turn, presages the themes Capote explored so brilliantly in *In Cold Blood*, and in his 1979 piece "Then It All Came Down," about Charles Manson's associate Bobby Beausoleil. On and on. By writing and working through, Capote, the spiritual waif as a child with no real fixed address, found his focus, or perhaps, mission: to articulate all that which his circumstances and society had hitherto not described, especially transience, and those moments of heterosexual love or closeted, silent homoeroticism, that sealed people off, one from the other. In the intermittenly touching "If I Forget You," a woman waits for love, or love's illusions, despite the reality of a situation. The piece is subjective; thwarted love always is. Capote further explores missed chances and forsaken love from a woman's point of view in "The Familiar Stranger." In it an elderly white woman named Nannie dreams she has a male visitor who is at once solicitous and menacing in the way that sex can sometimes feel. Like the first-person narrator in Katherine Anne Porter's masterly 1930 story "The Jilting of Granny Weatherall," Nannie's hardness—her voice of complaint—is the result of having been rejected, fooled by love, and the vulnerability it requires. Nannie's resulting skepticism spills out into the world—her world, being, in sum, her black retainer, Beulah.

Beulah is always there—supportive, sympathetic—and yet she has no face, no body: she is a feeling, not a person. Here again Capote fails his talent when it comes to race; Beulah is not a creation based on truth but the fiction of race, what a black woman is, or stands for. Urgently we look past Beulah to other Capote works for his brilliant sense of reality in fiction, that which gives the work its peculiar resonance. When Capote began publishing his nonfiction writing in the mid- to late 1940s, fiction writers rarely if ever crossed over into journalism—it was considered a lesser form, despite its importance to early masters of the English novel, such as Daniel DeFoe and Charles Dickens, both of whom had started off as reporters. (DeFoe's vexing and profound *Robinson Crusoe* was partly inspired by an explorer's journal and Dickens's 1853 masterpiece *Bleak House,* alternates subjective first-person narration with third-person journalistic-like reports about English law and society.) In short, it was rare for a modern writer of fiction to give up its relative freedoms for journalism's strictures, but I think Capote always loved the tension inherent in cheating the truth. He always wanted to elevate reality above the flatness of facts. (In his first novel, 1948's *Other Voices, Other Rooms,* the book's protagonist, Joel Harrison Knox, recognizes that impulse in himself. When the black servant Missouri catches Joel in a lie, she says, "You is a gret big story." Capote then goes on to write: "Somehow, spinning the tale, Joel had believed every word.") Later, in 1972's "Self-Portrait," we have this:

Q: Are you a truthful person?
A: As a writer—yes, I think so. Privately—well, that is a matter of opinion; some of my friends think that when relating an event or piece of

news, I am inclined to alter and overelaborate. Myself, I just call it making something "come alive." In other words, a form of art. Art and truth are not necessarily compatible bedfellows.

In his wonderful early nonfiction books—1950's *Local Color* and 1956's strange and hilarious *The Muses Are Heard*, which covers a troupe of black actors in communist-era Moscow performing *Porgy and Bess*, and the Russians sometimes-racist reaction to the performers—the writer used factual events as a jumping-off point to aid in his musings about outsiders. Most of his subsequent nonfiction work would be about out-siders, too—all those drifters and proles trying to make it in unfamiliar worlds. In "Swamp Terror" and "Mill Store," both from the early 1940s, the backwoods worlds Capote draws are political in shape. Each tale takes place in worlds limited by machismo and poverty and the confusion and shame that each can bring about. These pieces are the "shadow" of *Other Voices, Other Rooms*, which can best be read as a report from the emotional and racial terrain that helped form him. (Capote said that the book ended the first phase of his life as a writer. It is also a landmark in "out" literature. Essentially the novel asks what's different. In one scene Knox listens as a young girl goes on and on about her butch sister's desire to be a farmer. "What's wrong with that?" Joel asks. Indeed, what *is* wrong with that? Or any of it?) In *Other Voices, Other Rooms*, a work of high southern gothic symbolism and drama, we meet Missouri, or Zoo, as she is sometimes called. Unlike her literary predecessors she is not content to live in the shadows while emptying bedpans and listening to quarrelsome white folk in Capote's house of the sick. But Zoo can't break free; she's stopped in freedom's tracks by the machismo, ignorance, and brutality the author vividly describes in "Swamp Terror" and "Mill Store": After Zoo runs off, she's forced to return to her former life. There, Joel asks her if she managed to make it up north and see snow. Zoo shouts: "There ain't none. Hit's all a lotta foolery, snow and such: that sin! It's everywhere! . . . Is a nigger sun, an my soul, it's black." She's been raped and burned and her attackers were white. Despite the fact that Capote said he was not a political person ("I've never voted. Though, if invited, I suppose I might join almost anyone's protest parade: Antiwar, Free Angela, Gay Liberation, Ladie's Lib, etc."), politics was always part of his life because his soul was queer and he had to survive, which means being aware of how to use your difference, and why. As an artist, Truman Capote treated truth as a metaphor he could hide behind, the better to expose himself in a world not exactly congenial to a southern-born queen with a high voice who once said to a disapproving truck driver: "What are you looking at? I wouldn't kiss you for a dollar." So doing, he gave his readers, queer and not queer, license to imagine his real self in a real situation—in Kansas, researching *In Cold Blood*—while watching the TV because it's interesting to think about him maybe taking in news reports from the time, like that story about those four black girls in Alabama, one of his home states, blown to bits in a church by racism and maleficence, and maybe wondering how, as the author of 1958's *Breakfast at Tiffany's*, he could have written of Holly Golightly, the book's star, asking for a cigarette and then saying: "I don't mean you, O.J. You're such a slob. You always nigger-lip." Capote's best fiction is true to his queerness and it's weakest when he fails to throw off the mores of the only gay male model he probably knew when he was growing up in Louisiana and Alabama: a melancholy, arch, mired-in-nostalgia-and-honeysuckle queen named Cousin Randolph, who "understands" Zoo because her reality doesn't interfere with his narcissism—at least he wasn't *that*. By writing in and of his times, Capote transcended both by becoming an artist, one who presaged our time by delineating the truth to be had in fabrication.

HILTON ALS is a staff writer for *The New Yorker*. His work also appears in *The New York Review of Books*. He is the author of *The Women* and *White Girls*. He lives in New York.

Contents

Contents

The Early Stories of
TRUMAN CAPOTE

Parting of the Way

Parting of the Way

Twilight had come; the lights from the distant town were beginning to flash on; up the hot and dusty road leading from the town came two figures, one, a large and powerful man, the other, young and delicate.

Jake's flaming red hair framed his head, his eyebrows looked like horns, his muscles bulged and were threatening; his overalls were faded and ragged, and his toes stuck out through pieces of shoes. He turned to the young boy walking beside him and said, "Guess this is just about time to make camp for tonight. Here, kid, take this bundle and lay it over there; then git some wood—and make it snappy too. I want to make the vittels before it's all dark. We can't have anybody seein' us. Go on there, hurry up."

Tim obeyed the orders and set about gathering the

wood. His thin shoulders drooped from the strain, and his gaunt features stood out with protruding bones. His eyes were weak but sympathetic; his rose-bud mouth puckered slightly as he went about his labor.

Neatly he piled the wood while Jake cut strips of bacon and put them in a grease-coated pan. Then, when the wood was ready to be fired, he searched through his overalls for a match.

"Damn it, where did I put those matches? Where are they, you ain't got 'em, have you, kid? Nuts, I didn't think so; ah, here they are." He drew a paper of matches from a pocket, lit one, and protected the tiny flame with his rough hands.

Tim put the pan with the bacon over the small fire that was rapidly catching. The bacon remained still for a minute or so and then a tiny crackling sound started, and the bacon was frying. A very rancid odor came from the meat. Tim's sick face turned sicker from the fumes.

"Gee, Jake, I don't know whether I can eat any of this junk or not. It doesn't look right to me. I think it's rancid."

"You'll eat it or nothin'. If you weren't so stingy with that piece of change you got, we could a got us somethin' decent to eat. Why, kid, you got a whole ten bucks. It doesn't take that much to get home on."

"Yes, it does, I've got it all figured out. The train fare will cost me five bucks, and I want to get a new suit for about three bucks, then I want to git Ma somethin' pretty for about a dollar or so; and I figure my food will cost a buck. I want to git lookin' decent. Ma an' them don't know I been bummin' around the country for the last two years; they think I'm a traveling salesman—that's what I wrote them; they think I'm just coming home now to stay a while afore I start out on a little trip somewhere."

"I ought to take that money off you—I'm mighty hungry—I might take that piece of change."

Tim stood up, defiant. His weak, frail body was a joke compared to the bulging muscles of Jake. Jake looked at him and laughed. He leaned back against a tree and roared.

"Ain't you a pretty somethin'? I'd jes' twist that mess of bones you call yourself. Jes' break every bone in your body, only you been pretty good for me—stealin' stuff for me an' the likes of that—so I'll let you keep your pin money." He laughed again. Tim looked at him suspiciously and sat back down on a rock.

Jake took two tin plates from a sack, put three strips of the rancid bacon on his plate and one on Tim's. Tim looked at him.

"Where is my other piece? There were four strips. You're supposed to get two an' me two. Where is my other piece?" he demanded.

Jake looked at him. "I thought you said that you didn't want any of this rancid meat." Putting his hands on his hips he said the last eight words in a high, sarcastic, feminine voice.

Tim remembered, he had said that, but he was hungry, hungry and cold.

"I don't care. I want my other piece. I'm hungry. I could eat just about anything. Come on, Jake, gimme my other piece."

Jake laughed and stuck all the three pieces in his mouth.

Not another word was spoken. Tim went sulkily over in a corner, and, reaching out from where he was sitting, he gathered pine twigs, neatly laying them along the ground. Finally, when this job was finished, he could stand the strained silence no longer.

"Sorry, Jake, you know how it is. I'm excited about getting home and everything. I'm really very hungry too, but, gosh, I guess all there is to do is to tighten up my belt."

"The hell it is. You could take some of that jack you

got and go get us a decent meal. I know what you're thinkin'. Why don't we steal some food? But hell, you don't catch me stealin' anything in this burg. I heard from buddies that this place," he pointed a finger toward the lights that indicated a town, "is one of the toughest little burgs this side of nowhere. They watch bums like eagles."

"I guess you're right, but you understand, I just ain't goin' to take any chances on losin' none of this dough. It's got to last me, 'cause it's all I got an' all I'm liable to get in the next few years. I wouldn't disappoint Ma for anything in the world."

Morning came gloriously, the large orange disc known as the sun came up like a messenger from heaven over the distant horizon. Tim had awakened just in time to see the sunrise.

He shook Jake, who jumped up demanding: "What do you want? Oh! it's time to get up. Hell, how I hate to get up." Then he let out a mighty yawn and stretched his powerful arms as far as they would go.

"This is shore goin' to be one hot day, Jake. I shore am glad I ain't goin' to have to walk. That is, only as far back into that town as the railroad station is."

"Yeh, kid. Think of me, I ain't got any place to go,

but I'm goin' there, just walkin' in the hot sun. I wish it would always be like early spring, not too hot, not too cold. I sweat to death in summer and freeze in winter. It's a heck of a climate. I think I'd like to go to Florida in the winter, but there ain't no good pickins there anymore." He walked over and started to take out the frying utensils again. He reached into the pack and brought out a bucket.

"Here, kid, go up there to that farm house about a quarter of a mile up the road and git some water."

Tim took the bucket and started up the road.

"Hey, kid, ain't you goin' to take your jacket? Ain't you afraid I'll steal your dough?"

"Nope. I guess I can trust you." But down deep in his heart he knew that he couldn't. The only reason he hadn't turned back was because he didn't want Jake to know that he didn't trust him. The chances were that Jake knew it anyway.

Up the road he trudged. It was not paved, but even in the early morning the dust still stuck. The white house was just a little bit farther. As he reached the gate, he saw the owner coming out of the cow shed with a pail in his hand.

"Hey, Mister, can I please have this bucket filled with some water?"

"I guess so. There's the pump." He pointed a dirty finger toward a pump in the yard. Tim went in. He grasped the pump-handle and pushed it up and down. Suddenly the water came spilling out in a cold stream. He reached down and stuck his mouth to the spout and let cold liquid run in and over his mouth. After filling the bucket he started back down the road.

He broke his way through the brush and came back into the clearing. Jake was bending over the bag.

"Damn, they jes' ain't nothin' left to eat. I thought, at least, there were a couple of slices of that bacon left."

"Aw, that's all right. When I get to town I can get me a whole meal—an' maybe I'll buy you a cup of coffee—an' a bun."

"Gee, but you're generous." Jake looked at him disgustedly.

Tim picked up his jacket and reached in the pocket. He brought out a worn leather wallet and unfastened the catch.

"I'm about to produce the dough that's goin' to take me home." He repeated the words several times, caressing it each time.

He reached into the wallet. He brought out his hand—empty. An expression of horror and unbelief overcame him. Wildly he tore the wallet apart, then dashed about looking through the pine needles. Furiously he ran around like a trapped animal—then he saw Jake. His small thin frame shook with fury. Wildly he turned on him.

"Give me back my money, you thief, liar, you stole it from me. I'll kill you if you don't give it back. Give it back! I'll kill you! You promised you wouldn't take it. Thief, liar, cheat! Give it to me, or I'll kill you."

Jake looked at him astounded and said, "Why, Tim, kid, I ain't got it. Maybe you lost it, maybe it's still in those pine needles. Come on, we'll find it."

"No, it's not there. I've looked. You stole it. There jes' ain't anybody else who could of. You did it. Where did you put it? Give it back, you got it. . . . give it back!"

"I swear I haven't got it. I swear it by all the principles I got."

"You ain't got no principles. Jake, look me in the eyes and say you hope you get killed if you ain't got my money."

Jake turned around. His red hair seemed even redder in the bright morning light, his eyebrows more like thorns. His unshaven chin jutted out, and his yellow teeth showed at the far end of his upturned and twisted mouth.

"I swear that I ain't got your ten bucks. If I ain't tellin' the truth, I hopes that the next time I rides the rail I gets killed."

"Okay, Jake, I believe you. Only where could my money be? You know I ain't got it on me. If you ain't got it, where is it?"

"You ain't searched the camp yet. Look all 'round. It must be here somewheres. Come on, I'll help you look. It couldn' of walked off."

Tim ran nervously about, repeating: "What if I don't find it? I can't go home, I can't go home lookin' like this."

Jake went about the search only half heartedly, his big body bending and looking in the pine needles, in the sack. Tim took off his clothes and stood naked in the middle of the camp, tearing out the seams in his overalls searching for his money.

Near tears, he sat down on a log. "We might as well give it up. It ain't here. It ain't nowheres. I can't go home, and I want to go home. Oh! what will Ma say? Please, Jake, have you got it?"

Damn, you, for the last time NO! The next time you ask me that I'm agoin' to knock hell out o' you."

"Okay, Jake, I guess I'll just have to bum around

with you some more—'till I can get me enough money again to go home on—I can write Ma a card an' say that they sent me off on a trip already, an' I can come see her later."

"I shore ain't goin' to have you bummin' 'round with me anymore. I'm tired of kids like you. You'll have to go your own way an' find y'r own pickins."

Jake mused to himself. "I want the kid to come with me, but I shouldn'. Maybe if I leave him alone, he'll get wise an' go home an' make somethin' of himself. That's what he ought to do, go home an' tell the truth."

They both sat down on a log. Finally Jake said, "Kid, if you are goin' you better get started. Come on, get up, it's about seven already, an' got to get started."

Tim picked up his knapsack, and they walked out to the road together. Jake's big powerful figure looked fatherly beside Tim. It seemed as if he might be protecting a small child. They reached the road and turned to face each other to say goodbye.

Jake looked into Tim's clear, watery blue eyes. "Well, so long, kid, let's shake hands an' part friends."

Tim extended his tiny hand. Jake wrapped his paw over Tim's. He gave him a hearty shake—the kid allowed his hand to be moved limply. Jake let go—the kid felt a something in his hand. He opened it, and there lay the ten dollar bill. Jake was hurrying away, and Tim started after him. Perhaps it was just the bright sunlight reflecting on his eyes—and then again—perhaps it really was tears.

Mill Store

The woman gazed out of the back window of the Mill Store, her attention rapt upon the children playing happily in the bright water of the creek. The sky was completely cloudless, and the southern sun was hot on the earth. The woman wiped the sweat off her forehead with a red handkerchief. The water, rushing rapidly over the bright creek bottom pebbles, looked cold and inviting. If those picnickers weren't down there now, she thought, I swear I'd go and sit in that water and cool myself off. Whew—!

Almost every Saturday people would come from the town on picnic parties and spend the afternoon feasting on the white pebbled shores of Mill Creek, while their children waded in the semi-shallow water. This afternoon, a Saturday late in August, there was a Sunday school picnic in progress. Three elderly women, Sunday school teachers, rushed about the shady spot, anxiously tending their young charges.

The woman, watching from the Mill Store, turned her gaze back into the comparatively dark interior of the store and searched around for a pack of cigarettes. She was a big woman, dark and sunburned. Her black hair was thick but cut short. She was dressed in a cheap calico dress. As she lighted her cigarette she frowned over the smoke. She twisted her mouth and grimaced. That was the only trouble with this damn smoking; it hurt the ulcers in her mouth. She inhaled sharply, the suction easing the stinging sores for the moment.

It must be the water, she thought. I ain't used to drinkin' this well water. She had only come to the town three weeks ago, looking for a job. Mr. Benson had given her the job, a chance to work in the Mill Store. She didn't like it here. It was five miles to the town, and she wasn't exactly *prone* to walking. It was too quiet, and at night, when she heard the crickets chirping and the bull frogs croaking their lonely cry, she would get the "jitters."

She glanced at the cheap alarm clock. It was three-thirty, the loneliest, most interminable hour of the day for her. The store was a stuffy place, smelling of kerosene and fresh cornmeal and stale candies. She leaned back out the window. The August mid-afternoon sun hung hot in the sky.

The store was on a sharp red clay bank that rose straight from the creek. At one side there was a big crumbling mill that no one had used for six or seven years. A rickety, gray wood dam held out the pond waters from the creek which flowed like an opalescent olive ribbon through the woods. The picnickers had to pay a dollar at the store for the use of the grounds and for fishing in the pond above the dam. One day she had gone fishing at the pond but all she had caught were a couple of skinny, bony cat-fish and two moccasins. How she had screamed when she pulled the snakes up, twisting, flashing their slimy bodies in the sun, their poisonous, cotton mouths sunk into her hook. After the second one, she had dropped her pole and line, rushed back to the store and spent the rest of the humid day consoling herself with movie magazines and a bottle of bourbon.

She thought about it as she looked down at the children splashing in the water. She laughed a little, but just the same she was afraid of the slimy things.

Suddenly a shy young voice behind her said, "Miss—?"

She was startled; she jumped around with a fierce look in her eye. "Ya don't have to sneak—oh, what d'you want, Kid?"

A little girl pointed to an old fashioned glass show case, filled with cheap candies—jelly beans, gum drops, peppermint sticks, jaw-breakers scattered about the case. As the child pointed to each desired article the woman reached in and threw it in a small, brown paper bag. The woman watched the child intensely as she chose her purchases. She reminded her of someone. It was the child's eyes. They were bright, like bubbles of blue glass. Such a pale, sky blue. The little girl's hair dipped in waves almost down to her shoulders. It was fine, honey-colored hair. Her legs and face and arms were dark brown, almost too dark. The woman knew the child must have been out in the sun a great deal. She couldn't help staring at her.

The little girl looked up from her purchasing and asked shyly, "Is something wrong with me?" She looked around her dress to see if it was torn.

The woman was embarrassed. She looked down quickly and began to roll up the end of the bag. "Why, no—no—not at all."

"Oh, I thought there was because you was looking at me so funny." The child seemed reassured.

The woman leaned over the counter as she handed the bag to the little girl and touched her hair. She just had to; it seemed so rich, like sweet yellow butter.

"What's your name, Kid?" she asked.

The child looked frightened. "Elaine," she said. She grabbed the bag, laid some hot coins on the counter and hurried quickly out of the store.

"Bye, Elaine," the woman called, but the little girl was already out of the store and hurrying across the bridge to rejoin her playmates.

That's a helluva thing, she thought. That kid's eyes are just like his. Those damned eyes. She sat down in a chair in the corner of the store, took one last drag on the cigarette and crushed it lifeless on the bare floor. She pressed her head into her lap and fell into a hot semi-sleep. God, she thought as she dozed, those eyes and, she moaned, these damned ulcers.

She was awakened by four young boys shaking her shoulders and jumping around the store in a frenzy of excitement. "Wake up," they yelled. "Wake up."

She looked at them, bleary-eyed for a moment. Her cheeks were hot all over. The ulcers burned in her mouth. She swept them carelessly with her tongue.

"What'sa matter?" she asked, "What'sa matter?"

"Have you got a telephone or a car, Lady, please?" asked one of the excited boys.

"No, no I haven't," she said, now fully awake. "What's the matter? What's happened? Dam hasn't burst, has it?"

The boys jumped around. They were too excited to stand still; they just jumped around moaning, "Oh, what are we gonna do! She'll die, she'll die!"

The woman was getting mad. "What the hell's happened, anyway? Tell me, but quick!"

"A kid's been snake bit," sobbed a small, chubby boy.

"For God's sake, where?"

"Down in the creek," he pointed toward the window.

The woman rushed out the store. Across the bridge she flew and down the pebbled beach. A crowd of people were gathered at the end of the beach. One of the Sunday school teachers was flying around the crowd, yelling her head off. Some of the children stood to one side, wall-eyed with horror and amazement at this thing that had broken up their party.

The woman broke through the crowd and saw the child that lay on the sand. It was the girl with the bubble eyes, like bright blue glass. "Elaine," cried the woman. Everyone turned their attention on the new arrival. She knelt down beside the child and looked at the wound.

Already it was swelling and turning color. The child shivered and wept and hit her head with her hand.

"Haven't you got a car?" the woman asked one of the school teachers. "How did you get here?"

"We hiked over," the other woman answered, fear and bewilderment in her eyes.

The woman rang her hands in rage. "Look here," she said, "this kid's serious; she's liable to die."

They all only stared at her. What could they do? They were helpless, just three silly women and a lot of children.

"All right, all right," the woman cried. "You, you run up to the place and get a coupla chickens. You women get somebody to start running back to town to get a doctor. Hurry, hurry. We haven't got a minute to lose."

"But what can we do now for the child?" one of the women asked.

"I'll show you," the woman said.

She knelt down beside the little girl and looked at the wound. The place was swollen big now. Without a moment's hesitation the woman bent over and sunk her mouth against the wound. She sucked and sucked, letting up every few seconds and spitting out a mouthful of fluid. There were only a few children left and one of the teachers. They stared with horrified fascination and admiration. The child's face turned the color of chalk and she fainted. The woman spat out mouthfuls of saliva mixed with the poison. Finally she got up and ran to the stream. Rinsing her mouth out with the water, she gurgled furiously.

The children with the chickens arrived. Three big fat hens. The woman grabbed one of them by the legs, and with the aid of a jackknife ripped it open, the hot blood running over everything. "The blood draws what poison there is left, out," she explained.

When that chicken had turned green she ripped open another and placed it against the child's wound.

"Come on now," she said. "Get hold of her and carry her up to the store. We'll wait there until the doctor comes.

The children ran eagerly forward and with their combined efforts, managed to carry her comfortably. They were crossing the bridge when the school teacher said, "Really, I don't know how we can ever thank you. It was so, it was—"

The woman pushed her aside and hurried on up the bridge. The ulcers were burning like mad from the poison, and she felt sick all over when she thought of what she had done.

Hilda

"Hilda—Hilda Weber, will you please come here a moment?"

Quickly she went to the front of the room and stood next to Miss Armstrong's desk.

"Hilda," Miss Armstrong said quietly, "Mr. York would like to see you after dismissal."

Hilda stared questioningly for a moment, then she shook her head, her long black hair swinging from side to side and partly covering her pleasant face.

"Are you sure it's me, Miss Armstrong? I haven't done anything." Her voice was frightened but very mature for a sixteen-year-old girl.

Miss Armstrong seemed annoyed. "I can only tell you what this note says." She handed the tall girl a slip of white paper.

Hilda Weber—office—3:30.

Mr. York, Principal.

Hilda went slowly back to her desk. The sun shone brightly through the window and she blinked her eyes. Why was she being summoned to the office? It was the first time she had ever been called to see the principal, and she had been going to Mount Hope High for almost two years.

II

Somewhere in the back of her mind there was a vague fear. She had a feeling that she knew what it was the principal wanted to see her for—but no, that couldn't be it—no one knew, no one even suspected. She was Hilda Weber—hard working, studious, shy, and unassuming. No one knew. How could they?

She felt a little comforted. It must be something else that Mr. York wanted to see her about. Perhaps he wanted her to be on the committee for the Prom. She smiled feebly and picked up her big green Latin book.

When the dismissal bell rang, Hilda went directly

to Mr. York's office. She presented the note to the complacent secretary in the outer office. When she was told to go in, she thought her legs were going to crumple beneath her. She shook with nervousness and excitement.

Hilda had seen Mr. York in the school corridors and had heard him speak at school assemblies but she could never remember having actually spoken with him personally. He was a tall man with a thin face topped with a great spray of red hair. His eyes were sea-pale and, at the moment, extremely pleasant.

Hilda came into the small, modestly furnished office with troubled eyes and a pale face.

III

"You are Hilda Weber?" The words were more a statement than a question. Mr. York's voice was grave and pleasant.

"Yes, Sir, I am." Hilda was surprised at her own calm voice. Inside she was cold and jittery and her hands clasped her books so tightly that she could feel the warm sweat. There was something terrible and frightening about seeing a principal, but his friendly eyes disarmed her.

"I see by your record here," he picked up a big yellow card, "that you are an honor student, that you came here from a boarding school in Ohio, and that you are at present a Junior here at Mount Hope High School. Is that correct?" he asked.

She nodded her head and watched him intently.

"Tell me, Hilda, what are you most interested in?"

"In what way, Sir?" She must be on her guard.

"Why, pertaining to a future career in life." He had picked up a gold key chain from his desk and was twirling it around.

"Well I don't know, Sir. I thought I would like to be an actress. I've always had a great interest in dramatics." She smiled, and dropped her gaze from his thin face to the whirling blur of chain.

"I see," he said. "I ask this only because I would like to understand you. It's quite important that I understand you." He turned his chair around and sat up straight to the desk. "Yes, quite important." She noticed that his air of informality had dropped.

IV

She fidgeted with her books nervously. He hadn't said anything yet to accuse her, but she knew that her face was flushed; she felt very hot all over. Suddenly the closeness of the room was unbearable.

He laid down the chain. He was fixing to speak, she knew because she heard his sharp intake of breath, but she didn't dare look up at him because she knew what he was going to say.

"Hilda, I suppose you know there has been a great deal of thieving going on here in the girls' lockers." He paused a moment. "It's been going on for some time now—but we haven't been able to lay our hands on the girl who would steal from her class mates." He was stern and deliberate. "There is no place in this high school for a thief!" he said earnestly.

Hilda stared down at her books. She could feel her chin trembling and she bit her lips. Mr. York half rose from his seat and then sat down again. They sat in a tense, strained silence. Finally he reached in his desk drawer and pulled out a small blue box and emptied the contents on the desk. Two gold rings, a charm bracelet, and some coins.

"Do you recognize these?" he asked.

She stared at them for a long time. Fully forty-five seconds. They blurred in front of her eyes.

"But I didn't steal those things, Mr. York, if that's what you mean!"

V

He sighed. "They were found in your locker, and besides—we've had our eye on you for some time!"

"But I didn't—" she stopped short, it was hopeless.

Finally Mr. York said, "But what I can't understand is why a child like you would want to do such a thing. You're bright, and as far as I can find out, you come from a fine family. Frankly, I am completely baffled."

She still sat silent, fumbling with her books, and feeling as if the walls were close and tight, as if something were trying to smother her.

"Well," he continued, "if you aren't going to offer any explanation, I'm afraid there is little I can do for you. Don't you realize the seriousness of this offense?"

"It's not that," she rasped. "It's not that I don't want to tell you why I stole those things—it's just that I don't know how to tell you, because I don't know myself." Her slim shoulders shook, she was trembling violently.

He looked at her face—how hard to punish frailty in a child. He was visibly moved, he knew. He walked to the window and adjusted the shade.

The girl got up. She was overcome with a nauseous hate for this office and those bright shining trinkets on the desk. She could hear Mr. York's voice, it seemed far and distant.

VI

"This is a very serious matter, I'm afraid I will have to see your parents."

Her eyes leaped with fear. "You aren't going to have to tell my—?"

"Of course," Mr. York answered.

Suddenly she didn't care anymore about anything except getting out of this little white office with its ugly furnishings and its red-headed occupant and the rings and bracelet and money. She hated them!

"You may go now."

"Yes, Sir."

When she left the office, he was occupied with putting the trinkets back in the little blue box. She walked slowly through the outer office and down the long empty corridor and out into the bright sunlight of the April afternoon.

Then, suddenly, she began to run, and she ran faster and faster. Down the high school street, and into the town and down the long main street. She didn't care if people did stare at her; all she wanted was to get as far away as she could. She ran away to the other side of town and into the park. There were only a few women there with their baby carriages. She collapsed onto one of the empty benches and hugged her aching side. After a while, it stopped hurting. She opened her big green Latin book, and behind its protective covers, began to cry softly, unconsciously fingering the gold key chain in her lap.

Miss Belle Rankin

I was eight the first time I saw Miss Belle Rankin. It was a hot August day. The sun was waning in the scarlet-streaked sky, and the heat was rising dry and vibrant from the earth.

I sat on the steps of the front porch, watching an approaching negress, and wondered how she could ever carry such a huge bundle of laundry on the top of her head. She stopped and in reply to my greeting, laughed, that dark, drawling negro laughter. It was then Miss Belle came walking slowly down the opposite side of the street. The washerwoman saw her, and as if suddenly frightened stopped in the middle of a sentence and moved hurriedly on to her destination.

I stared long and hard at this passing stranger who could cause such odd behavior. She was small and

clothed all in black, dusty and streaked—she looked un-
believably old and wrinkled. Thin gray wisps of hair lay
across her forehead, wet with perspiration. She walked
with her head down and stared at the unpaved sidewalk,
almost as if she were looking for something she had lost.
An old black and tan hound followed her, moving aim-
lessly in the traces of his mistress.

I saw her many times afterwards, but that first vision,
almost like a dream, will always remain the clearest—
Miss Belle, walking soundlessly down the street, little
clouds of red dust rising about her feet as she disappeared
into the dusk.

A few years later I was sitting in Mr. Joab's corner
drugstore, swigging on one of Mr. Joab's special milk
shakes. I was down at one end of the counter, and up at
the other sat two of the town's well-known drugstore
cowboys and a stranger.

This stranger was much more respectable in appearance than the people who usually came into Mr. Joab's.
But it was what he was saying in a slow, husky voice, that
caught my attention.

"Do you boys know anybody around here with some
nice Japonica trees for sale? I'm collecting some for an
Eastern woman building a place over in Natchez."

The two boys looked at one another, and then one of them, who was fat with huge eyes and fond of taunting me, said, "Well, I tell you, Mister, the only person I know of around here that has some real purty ones is a queer old doll, Miss Belle Rankin—she lives about a half mile out from here in a right weird lookin' place. It's old and run down, built sometime before the Civil War. Mighty queer, though, but if Japonicas is what you're lookin' for, she's got the nicest I ever peeked at."

"Yeah," piped up the other boy, who was blond and pimply, and the fat boy's stooge. "She oughta sell them to you. From what I hear she's starvin' to death out there—ain't got nothin' 'ccpt an old nigger that lives on the place and hoes around in a weed patch they call the garden. Why, the other day I hear, she walked into the Jitney Jungle market and went around pickin' out the old spoiled vegetables and makin' Olie Peterson give 'em to her. Queerest lookin' witch you ever seen—looks like she might be a hunnerd in the shade. The niggers are so scared of her—"

But the stranger interrupted the boy's torrent of information and asked, "Well then, you think she might sell?"

"Sure," said the fat boy, with the smirk of certain knowledge on his face.

The man thanked them and started to walk out, then suddenly turned around and said, "How would you boys like to ride out there and show me where it is? I'll bring you back afterwards."

The two loafers quickly assented. That kind was always anxious to be seen in cars, especially with strangers; it made it seem like they had connections, and, anyway, there were the inevitable cigarettes.

It was about a week later when I went into Mr. Joab's again that I heard how it turned out.

The fat one was narrating with much fervor to an audience consisting of Mr. Joab and myself. The more he talked the louder and more dramatic he became.

"I tell you that old witch should be run out of town. She's crazy as a loon. First of all, when we get out there she tries to run us off the place. Then she sends that queer old hound of hers after us. I'll bet that thing's older than she is. Well, anyway, the mutt tried to take a hunk out of me, so I kicked him right square in the teeth— then she starts an awful howl. Finally that old nigger of hers gets her quieted down enough so that we can talk to her. Mr. Ferguson, that was the stranger, explained how he wanted to buy her flowers, you know those old Japonica trees. She says she never heard of such goin's on; besides, she wouldn't sell any of her trees because she liked them better than anything else she had. Now, wait till you catch this—Mr. Ferguson offered her two hundred dollars just for one of those trees. Can you tie that—two hundred bucks! That old goat told him to get off the place—so, finally we saw that it was hopeless, so we left. Mr. Ferguson was purty disappointed, too; he was really countin' on getting them trees. He said they were some of the finest he had ever seen."

He leaned back and took a deep breath, exhausted by his long recital.

"Damn," he said, "what does anybody want with those old trees and at two hundred berries a throw? That ain't corn."

When I left Mr. Joab's, I thought about Miss Belle all the way home. I had often wondered about her. She seemed too old to be alive—it must be terrible to be that old. I could not see why she wanted the Japonicas so badly. They were beautiful, but if she was so poor—well, I was young, and she was very old with little left in life. I was so young that I never thought that I would ever be old, that I could ever die.

* * *

It was the first of February. Dawn had broken dull and gray with streaks of pearl-white across the sky. Outside, it was cold and still with intermittent gusts of hungry wind eating at the gray, leafless limbs of the huge trees surrounding the decaying ruins of the once majestic "Rose Lawn," where Miss Rankin lived.

The room was cold when she awoke and long tears of ice hung on the eaves of the roof. She shuddered a little as she looked about at the drabness. With an effort she slipped from beneath the gay colored scrap quilt.

Kneeling at the fireplace, she lit the dead branches that Len had gathered the day before. Her small hand, shrunken and yellow, fought with the match and the scraped surface of the limestone block.

After awhile the fire caught; there was the cracking of the wood and the rush of leaping flames, like the rattle of bones. She stood for a moment by the warm blaze and then moved uncertainly towards the frozen wash basin.

When she was dressed, she went to the window. It was beginning to snow, the thin watery snow that falls in a Southern winter. It melted as soon as it hit the ground, but Miss Belle, thinking of her long walk to town that day for food, felt a little dizzy and ill. Then she gasped, for she saw down below that the Japonicas were blooming; they were more beautiful than she had ever seen them. The vivid red petals were frozen and still.

Once, she could remember, years ago when Lillie was a little girl, she had picked huge baskets of them, and filled the lofty, empty rooms of Rose Lawn with their subtle fragrance and Lillie had stolen them and given them away to the negro children. How mad she had been! But now she smiled as she remembered. It had been at least twelve years since she had seen Lillie.

Poor Lillie, she's an old woman herself now. I was just nineteen when she was born and I was young and pretty. Jed used to say I was the most beautiful girl he had ever known—but that was so long ago. I can't remember exactly when I started being like this. I can't remember when I was first poor—when I started getting old. I guess it was after Jed went away—I wonder what ever happened to him. He just up and said to me that I was ugly and worn and he left, left me all alone except for Lillie— and Lillie was no good—no good—

She put her hands over her face. It still hurt to remember, and yet, almost every day she remembered these same things and sometimes it drove her mad and she would yell and scream, like the time the man came with those two jeering oafs, and wanted to buy her Japonicas; she would not sell them, never. But she was afraid of the man; she was afraid he would steal them and what could she do—people would laugh. And that was why she had screamed at them; that was why she hated them all.

Len came into the room. He was a small negro, old and stooped, with a scar across his forehead.

"Miss Belle," he asked in a wheezy voice, "were you gwine to town? I wouldn't go if I was you, Miss Belle. It's mighty nasty out there today." When he spoke, a gust of smoky steam came out of his mouth into the cold air.

"Yes, Len, I have to go to town today. I'm goin' in a little while; I want to be back before it's dark."

Outside, the smoke from the ancient chimney rose in lazy curling clouds and hung above the house in a blue fog, as if it were frozen—then was whirled away in a gust of bitter wind!

It was quite dark when Miss Belle started climbing up the hill towards home. Dark came quickly on these winter days. It came so suddenly today that it frightened her at first. There was no glowing sunset, only the pearl grayness of the sky deepening into rich black. The snow was still falling and the road was slushy and cold. The wind was stronger and there was the sharp cracking of dead limbs. She bent under the weight of her heavy basket. It had been a good day. Mr. Johnson had given her almost one-third of a ham and that little Olie Peterson had had quite a few unsalable vegetables. She would not have to go back for at least two weeks.

When she reached the house, she stopped a minute for breath, letting the hamper slip to the ground. Then, she walked to the edge of the land and started picking some of the huge rose-like Japonicas; she crushed one against her face but she did not feel its touch. She gathered an arm load and started back to the hamper, when suddenly she thought she heard a voice. She stood still and listened, but there was only the wind to answer.

She felt herself slipping down and could not help it; she grabbed into the darkness for support, but there was only emptiness. She tried to cry out for help but no sound came. She felt great waves of emptiness sweeping over her; fleeting scenes swept through her. Her life—utter futility and a momentary glimpse of Lillie, of Jed, and a sharp picture of her mother with a long lean cane.

I remember it was a cold winter day when Aunt Jenny took me down to the old run down place where Miss Belle lived. Miss Belle had died during the night and an old colored fellow that lived there on the place had found her. Just about everybody in town was going out to have a look. They hadn't moved her yet because the coroner hadn't given permission. So we saw her just as she had died. It was the first time I had ever seen a dead person and I'll never forget it.

She was lying in the yard by those Japonica trees of hers. All the wrinkles were smoothed on her face, and the bright flowers were scattered all over.

She looked so small and really young. There were little flakes of snow in her hair and one of those flowers was pressed close against her cheek. I thought she was one of the most beautiful things that I had ever seen.

Everybody said how sad it was and everything, but I thought this was strange as they were the ones who used to laugh and make jokes about her.

Well, Miss Belle Rankin was certainly an odd one and probably a little touched, but she really looked lovely that cold February morning with that flower pressed against her cheek and lying there so still and quiet.

If I Forget You

Grace had stood waiting on the porch for him for almost an hour. When she had seen him down in town that afternoon he had said he would be there at eight. It was almost eight-ten. She sat down in the porch swing. She tried not to think of his coming or even to look down the road in the direction of his house. She knew that if she thought about it, it would never happen. He just wouldn't ever come.

"Grace, are you still out there, hasn't he come yet?"

"No, Mother."

"Well you can't sit out there for the rest of the night, come right back into this house."

She didn't want to go back in, she didn't want to have to sit in that stuffy old living room and watch her father read the news and her mother work the cross word puzzles. She wanted to stay out here in the night where she could breathe and smell and touch it. It seemed so palpable to her that she could feel its texture like fine blue satin.

"Here he comes now, Mother," she lied, "he's coming up the road now, I'm going to run and meet him."

"You'll do nothing of the sort, Grace Lee," said her mother's sonorous voice.

"Yes, Mother, yes! I'll be back as soon as I say goodbye."

She tripped down the porch steps and out into the road before her mother could say anything more.

She had made up her mind that she was going to just keep right on walking until she met him, even if she had to walk all the way to his house. This was a big night for her, not exactly a happy one, but it was a beautiful one anyway.

He was going to leave town, after all these years. It would seem so funny after he was gone. She knew nothing would ever be quite the same again. Once in school, when Miss Saaron asked the pupils to write a poem, she had written a poem about him, it was so good that it had been published in the town paper. She had called it "In the Soul of the Night." She recited the first two lines as she sauntered along the moon drenched road.

My loves is a Bright Strong light,
That shuts out the darkness of the Night.

Once he had asked her if she really loved him. She had said, "I love you for now, but we're just kids, this is just puppy love." But she knew she had lied, at least lied to herself, for now, for this brief moment, she knew that she loved him and then only a month ago she was quite sure it was all very childish and silly. But now that he was going away she knew this was not so. Once he had told her, after the poem episode, that she shouldn't take it so seriously, after all she was only sixteen. "Why, by the time we're twenty, if someone was to mention our names to one another we probably wouldn't even recognize the name." She had felt terrible about that. Yes, he would probably forget her. And now he was going away and she might never see him again. He might become a great engineer just like he wanted to be, and she'd still be sitting down here in a little southern town no one ever heard of. "Maybe he won't forget me," she told herself. "Maybe he'll come back to me and take me away from here to some big place like New Orleans or Chicago or even New York." It made her wild eyed with happiness just to think of it.

The smell of the pine woods on either side of the road made her think of all the good times they had had picnicking and horseback riding and dancing.

She remembered the time he had asked her to go to the junior prom with him. That was when she had first known him. He was so awfully good looking and she was so proud of herself, no one would have ever thought that little Grace Lee with her green eyes and freckles would ever have walked off with a prize like him. She had been so proud and so excited that she had almost forgotten how to dance. She had been so embarrassed when she mistook the lead and he had stepped on her foot and torn her silk stocking.

And just when she had convinced herself that this was real romance her mother had gone and said that they were just children and after all children just couldn't possibly know what real "affection" was, as she termed it.

Then the girls in town, who were purple with envy, started a "We Don't Like Grace Lee Campaign." "Look at the little fool," they would whisper, "just throwing herself at him." "Why she's no better than a—than a—harlot." "I'd give a pretty penny to know what those two have been up to, but I suppose it would be too shocking for my ears."

Her pace quickened, she got mad just when she thought of it, those smug little prigs. She never would forget the fight she had had with Louise Beavers the time she had caught her reading a letter she had written aloud to a lot of laughing girls in the school wash room. Louise had stolen the letter out of one of Grace's books and she was reading it aloud to them all with great, mocking gestures, and making a joke out of something that wasn't funny at all.

"Oh, well, that's just a lot of trivial nonsense anyway," she thought.

The moon shone brightly in the sky, pale, wan little clouds hung around the surface like a fine lace shawl. She stared at it. She would soon be at his house. Just up this hill and down and there she would be. It was a fine little house, it was solid and substantial. It was just the perfect place for him to live, she thought.

Sometimes she thought it was just a lot of sentiment, this puppy love, but now she was certain that it wasn't. He was going to leave. He was going away to live with his aunt in New Orleans. His aunt was an artist, she did not like that very much. She had heard that artists were queer people.

He had not told her until yesterday that he was leaving. He must have been a little afraid too, she thought, and now I'm the one that's afraid. Oh, how happy everyone would be now that he was leaving and she wouldn't have him anymore, she could just see their laughing faces.

She brushed the light blonde hair out of her eyes. There was a cool wind blowing through the tree tops. She was nearing the crest of the hill, and suddenly she knew that he was coming up the other side and that they were going to meet at the top. She grew hot all over so sure was her premonition. She did not want to cry, she wanted to smile. She felt in her pocket for the picture of herself he had asked her to bring. It was a cheap snapshot that a man had taken of her at a carnival that had passed through the town. It didn't even look much like her.

Now that she was almost there she didn't want to go any further. As long as she hadn't actually said goodbye she still had him. She went and sat in the soft evening grass by the side of the road to wait for him.

"All I hope for," she said as she stared up into the dark, moon filled sky, "is that he doesn't forget me, I suppose that's all I have a right to hope for."

The Moth in the Flame

All afternoon Em had lain on the steel-framed bed. She had a scrap quilt pulled over her legs. She was just lying there and thinking. The weather had turned cold, even for Alabama.

George and all the other men from over the countryside were out looking for crazy old Sadie Hopkins. She had escaped from the jail. Poor old Sadie, thought Em, runnin' all over in those swamps and fields. She used to be such a pretty girl—just got mixed up with the wrong folks, I guess. Gone plumb crazy.

Em looked out the window of her cabin; the sky was dark and slate gray and the fields looked as if they had been frozen into furrows. She pulled the quilt closer about her. It certainly was lonesome out in this country, not another farm for four miles, fields on one side, swamp and woods on the other. She felt that maybe she had been born to be lonesome just as some people are born blind or deaf.

She stared around the small room, the four walls closing in around her. She sat silent, listening to the cheap alarm clock, tick-tock, tick-tock.

Suddenly the strangest feeling crept up her back, a feeling of fear and horror. She felt her scalp tingle. She knew, like a flash of blinding light, that there was someone watching her, someone standing very near and watching her with cold, calculating, insane eyes.

For a moment she lay so still that she could hear the pounding of her heart, and the clock sounded like a sledge hammer beating against a hollow stump. Em knew that she wasn't imagining things; she knew there was some cause for this fright; she knew by instinct, an instinct so clear and vital that it filled her whole body.

Slowly she got up and gazed about the room. She saw nothing; yet she felt that there was someone staring at her, following her every move.

She picked up the first thing that she touched, a stick of lighting wood. Then she called in a bold voice, "Who is it? What do you want?"

Only cold silence met her questions. Despite the actual physical cold she grew hot all over; she felt her cheeks burning.

"I know you're here," she screamed hysterically. "What do you want? Why don't you show yourself? Come out, you sneakin'—"

Then she heard a voice, tired and frightened, behind her.

"It's only me, Em—Sadie, you know, Sadie Hopkins."

Em whirled around. The woman who stood in front of her was half naked, her hair hanging wildly about her scratched and bruised face. Her legs were all marked with blood.

"Em," she pleaded, "please help me. I'm tired and hungry. Hide me someplace. Don't let them catch me, please don't. They'll lynch me; they think I'm crazy. I'm not crazy; you know that, Em. Please, Em." She was crying.

Em was too shocked and dazed to reply. She stumbled and sat down on the edge of the bed. "What are you doin' in here, Sadie? How did you get in?"

"I came through the back door," the crazy woman answered. "I've got to hide someplace. They're headin' this way through the swamps and they'll find him soon.

Oh, I didn't mean to do it; I didn't mean it, Em. The Lord knows I didn't mean it."

Em looked at her blankly. "What are you talkin' about?" she asked.

"That Henderson boy," cried Sadie. "He caught up with me in the woods. He was holdin' me and clawin' me and screamin' for the others. I didn't know what to do; I was scared. I tripped him; he fell over backwards, and I jumped on him and hit him in the head with a big rock. I just couldn't seem to stop hittin' him. I only meant to knock him out, but when I looked—OH, GOD!"

Sadie leaned back against the door, and began to chuckle and then to laugh. Soon the whole room was filled with wild, hysterical laughter. The dusk had fallen, and the bright flames from the limestone fireplace played weird shadows around the room. They danced in the blackness of the insane woman's eyes; they seemed to lash her hysteria into a wilder frenzy.

Em sat on the bed, horrified and dazed, her eyes filled with bewilderment and terror. She was hypnotized by Sadie, and her dark, evil laughter.

"But you'll let me stay, won't you, Em?" the woman shrieked. Then she looked into Em's eyes. She stopped laughing. "Please, Em," she begged. "I don't want them to catch me. I don't want to die; I want to live. They've done this to me; they've made me the way I am."

She looked into the fire. She knew that she would have to go. Then presently she asked, "Em, what part of the swamp aren't they going to cover today?"

Deliberately Em sat up, her eyes burning with hysterical tears. "They aren't goin' to cover the Hawkins' section till tomorrow." When she had told the lie, she felt her stomach sink; she felt as if she were falling through a thousand years.

"Goodbye, Em."

"Goodbye, Sadie."

Sadie walked out of the front door and Em watched her until she reached the edge of the swamp and disappeared into its dark jungle-like depths.

Part II

Em collapsed onto the bed and began to cry. She cried until she fell into a feverish sleep. She was awakened by the sound of men talking. She looked out into the dark yard and saw George and Hank Simmons and Bony Yarber coming toward the house.

Quickly she jumped up, got a wet cloth, and wiped her face. She turned up a lamp in the kitchen and was sitting reading when the men came in.

"Hello, honey," said George, depositing a kiss on her cheek. "Gosh, but you're hot. Are you feelin' all right?"

She nodded her head.

"Hello, Em," said the other two men.

She didn't bother to return their salutation. She sat reading. They each took a drink of water from the dipper.

"Boy, that sure tastes good," said George, "but how about somethin' with a little more punch to it, eh, boys?" He nudged Bony.

Suddenly Em laid down her magazine. Cautiously she looked around at them.

"Did—did," her voice quavered a little bit, "did you find Sadie?"

"Yes," answered George, "we found her in one of those whirlpools over in Hawkins' mirey part of the swamp. She'd drowned, committed suicide, I guess. But let's don't talk about it; it was God-awful. It was—"

But he didn't finish. Em jumped up from the table, knocked the lamp over, and ran into the bedroom.

"Now, what the hell do you suppose is eatin' her, I wonder," said George.

Swamp Terror

"Well, I'm shore tellin' you, Jep, you just ain't got the sense you wuz born with if you gonna go on in these woods lookin' for that convict."

The boy who spoke was small, with a nut-brown face covered with freckles. He looked eagerly at his companion.

"Listen here," Jep said. "I know very well whut I'm doin'—an' I don't need none of yo' advice or none of yo' sassy mouth."

"Boy, I do believe you is crazy. Whut would yo' ma say if she was to know you was out here in these spooky ol' woods lookin' fo' some ol' convict?"

"Lemmie, I'm not askin' fo' none of yo' mouth, an' I sho' ain't askin' fo' you to be taggin' along here with me. Now you can go on back—Pete an' I will go on and find that ol' buzzard—then we two, just us two, will go down an' tell those searchin' parties where he be. Won't we, Pete, ol' boy?" He patted a brown-and-tan dog trotting along by his side.

They walked on a little farther in silence. The boy called Lemmie was undecided what to do. The woods were dark and so quiet. Occasionally a bird would flutter or sing in the trees, and when their path ran near the stream they could hear it moving swiftly along over the rocks and tiny waterfalls. Yes, indeed, it was too quiet. Lemmie hated the thought of walking back to the edge of the woods alone, but he hated the idea of going on with Jep even worse.

"Well, Jep," he said finally, "I guess I'll just mosey on back. I'm shore not goin' on into this place any farther, not with all these trees an' bushes every place that ol' convict could hide behind, an' jump on you, an' kill you deader'n an ol' doorknob."

"Aw, go on back, you big sissy. I hope he gits you while you is goin' back thru' the ol' woods by yuhself."

"Well, so long—I guess I'll be seein' you in school tomorrow."

"Maybe. So long."

Jep could hear Lemmie running back through the

underbrush, his feet scurrying like a scared rabbit. "That's what he is," thought Jep, "just a scared rabbit. What a baby Lemmie is. We never should have brought him along with us, should we've, Pete?"

He demanded the last vocally, and the old brown-and-tan dog, perhaps frightened by the silence being too suddenly interrupted, let out a quick, scared, little bark.

They walked on in silence. Every now and then Jep would stop and stand listening attentively into the forest. But he heard not the slightest sound to indicate a presence trespassing here, other than his own. Sometimes they would come to a cleared place carpeted with soft green moss and shaded by big magnolia trees covered with large white blossoms—smelling of death.

"I guess maybe I should've listened to Lemmie. It shore 'nuff is spooky down in here." He stared up into the tops of the trees, every now and then seeing patches of blue. It was so dark here in this part of the woods— almost like night. Suddenly he heard a whirring sound. Almost in that second he recognized it; he stood paralyzed with fear—then Pete let out a short, horrible, little yelp. It broke the spell. He turned around, and there was a big rattlesnake poised to strike a second time. Jep jumped as far as he could, tripped, and fell flat on his face. Oh God! This was the end! He forced his eyes to look around, expecting to see the snake whirling through the air at him, but when his eyes finally came into focus, nothing was there. Then he saw the tip of a tail and a long cord of singing buttons crawling into the undergrowth.

For several minutes he couldn't move, he was so dazed by shock, and his body was numb with terror. Finally he raised up on his elbow and looked for Pete, but Pete wasn't anywhere in sight. He jumped up and began to search frantically for the dog. When he found him, Pete had rolled down a red gulley and was lying dead at the bottom, all stiff and swollen. Jep didn't cry; he was too frightened for that.

Now what would he do? He didn't know where he was. He began to run and then to tear madly through the forest, but he couldn't find the path. Oh, what was the use? He was lost. Then he remembered the stream, but that was useless. It ran through the swamp, and in parts it was too deep to wade; and in the summer it was sure to be infested with moccasins. Darkness was coming on, and the trees began to throw grotesque shadows about him.

"How does that ol' convict stand it in here?" he

thought. "Oh, my God, the convict! I forget all 'bout him. I've got to get out of this place."

He ran on and on. Finally he came to one of the cleared spots. The moon was shining right in the center. It looked like a cathedral.

"Maybe if I climb a tree," he thought, "I can see the field an' figger out a way to get there."

He looked around for the tallest of the trees. It was a straight, slick sycamore, with no branches near the bottom. But he was a good climber. Maybe he could make it.

He clasped the trunk of the tree with his strong, little legs and began to pull himself upward, inch by inch. He would climb two feet and slip down one. He kept his head strained back, looking up at the nearest branch he could clasp. When he reached it, he grabbed it and let his legs dangle free from the tree trunk. For a minute he thought he was going to fall, dangling there in space. Then he swung his leg over the next limb and sat astraddle it, panting for breath. After awhile he continued on up, climbing, limb after limb. The ground got farther and farther away. When he reached the top, he stuck his head up over the tree top and looked around, but he could see nothing except trees, trees everywhere.

He descended to the broadest and the strongest of

the tree limbs. He felt safe up here, with the ground so far away. Up here no one could see him. He would have to spend the night in the tree. If only he could stay awake and not fall asleep. But he was so tired that everything seemed to be whirling around and around. He shut his eyes for a minute and almost lost his balance. He came out of his trance with a start and slapped his cheeks.

It was so quiet, he couldn't even hear the crickets nor the bull frogs' nightly serenade. No, everything was quiet and frightening and mysterious. What was that? He jumped with a start; he heard voices; they were coming close; they were almost upon him! He looked down to the earth and he could see two figures moving in the underbrush. They were coming towards the clearing. Oh, oh, thank God! It must be some of the searchers.

But then he heard one of the voices, tiny and frightened, scream: "Stop! Oh please, please lemme go! I want to go home!"

Where had Jep heard that voice before? Of course, it was Lemmie's voice!

But what was Lemmie doing way down here in these woods? He had gone home. Who had him? All these thoughts ran through Jep's mind; then suddenly the realization of what was happening dawned on him. The escaped convict had Lemmie!

A voice, deep and threatening, split the air: "Shut up, you brat!"

He could hear Lemmie's scared sobbing. Their voices were quite clear now; they were almost directly under the tree. Jep held his breath with fear. He could hear his heart pound, and he could feel the ache of his stomach's knotted muscles.

"Sit down here, kid," the convict commanded, "and stop that damn cryin'!"

Jep could see that Lemmie fell helplessly to the ground and rolled over on the soft moss, trying desperately to stifle his sobs.

The convict was still standing. He was big and bulged with muscles. Jep could not see his hair; it was covered with a massive straw hat—the kind the convicts wear when they are working on the chain gang.

"Now tell me, kid," he demanded of Lemmie by shoving him, "how many people are there out lookin' for me?"

Lemmie didn't say a thing.

"Answer me!"

"I don't know," Lemmie answered faintly.

"All right. O.K. But tell me—what parts of the woods have they already covered?"

"I don't know."

"Aw, damn you." The convict slapped Lemmie across the cheek. Lemmie broke into renewed hysterics.

"Oh, no! No! This can't be happening to me," Jep thought. "It's all a dream, a nightmare. I'll wake up and find out that it ain't so."

He shut his eyes and opened them, in a physical attempt to prove that it was all just a nightmare. But there they were, the convict and Lemmie; and here he was, perched in the tree, scared even to breathe. If only he had something heavy, he could drop it on top of the convict's head and knock him cold. But he didn't have anything. He stopped his thoughts in mid-passage, for the convict was speaking again.

"Well, come on, kid; we can't stay here all night. The moon's goin' out, too—must be goin' to rain." He scanned the sky through the tree tops.

Jep's blood froze with terror; it seemed as if he was looking right at him; he was looking right at the branch he was sitting on. Any minute he would see him. Jep closed his eyes. The seconds pounded past like hours. When he finally got up the courage to look again, he saw that the convict was trying to pick Lemmie up off the ground. He hadn't seen him, thank God!

The convict said: "Come on, kid, before I cuff yuh a good one."

He was holding Lemmie half way up, like a sack of potatoes. Then suddenly he dropped him. "Shut up that cryin'!" he screamed at him. So electrifying was the tone of his voice that Lemmie stopped dead still. Something was the matter. The convict was standing by the tree, listening attentively into the forest.

Then Jep heard it, too. Something was coming through the undergrowth. He heard twigs snapping and bushes being scraped past. From where he was sitting he could see what it was. There were ten men closing in a circle around the clearing. But the convict could only hear the noise. He wasn't sure what it was; he became panicky.

Lemmie yelled, "Here we are! Here—Over he—!" But the convict had grabbed him; he was furtively pressing Lemmie's face into the ground. The little body was squirming and kicking, and then, all of a sudden, it went limp and lay very still. Jep saw the convict take his hand off the back of the boy's head. Something was the matter with Lemmie. Then Jep saw it in a flash; it was like something he just knew—Lemmie was dead! The convict had smothered him to death!

The men were no longer creeping in; they broke through the underbrush furiously. The convict saw he was trapped; he backed up against the trunk of Jep's tree and began to whine.

And then it was all over. Jep yelled and the men held their arms to catch him. He jumped and landed, unharmed, in the arms of one of the men.

The convict was handcuffed and crying. "That damned kid! It was all his fault!"

Jep looked over at Lemmie. One of the men was bending over him. Jep heard him turn to a man by his side and say, "Yep, he's dead all right."

It was then that Jep began to laugh; he laughed hysterically, and hot salty tears ran down his cheeks.

The Familiar Stranger

"And Beulah," Nannie called, "before you go, come in here and fix my pillows, this rocking chair's awfully uncomfortable."

"Yes, ma'am, ah'll be right there."

Nannie sighed heavily. She picked up the paper and thumbed through the first sheets to the society section—or social column as there wasn't any real society in Collinsville.

"Let's see now," she said, adjusting her horn rimmed glasses over her proud nose. " 'Mr. and Mrs. Yancey Bates go to Mobile to visit relatives.' Not nothin' much to that, people are always visiting each other," she mused half aloud. She turned down to the death notices, it always gave her a grim pleasure to read them. Day by day the people she had known all her life, the men and women she had grown up with, they were all dying. She was proud that she was still alive while they lay cold and still in their graves.

Beulah came into the room. She came over to the rocker in which Miss Nannie sat reading the paper. She took the pillows out from behind the aging woman's back, puffed them up and arranged them comfortably again behind her mistress's back.

"That feels much better, Beulah. You know I get this rheumatism every time about this year. It's so painful and I do feel so helpless, yes, indeed, so helpless."

Beulah nodded agreeingly, sympathetically.

"Yes, ma'am, ah knows just how it be. Ah had an uncle once near 'bout died from it."

"I see here in the paper, Beulah, where old Will Larson died. Funny no one has called me up or told me about it. He used to be a friend of mine, you know, Beulah, a very good friend." She nodded her head waggishly, implying, of course, that he had been one of her legion of phantom admirers.

"Well," said Beulah, glancing at the big grandfather clock that stood against the wall, "ah guess ah bettah be goin' on down to the doctah's to get yo medicine. Just you stay there and ah'll be back real quick."

She disappeared out the door and in about five minutes Nannie heard the front door slam. She glanced over the paper once more. She tried to get interested in the editorial, she tried the article about the proposed new furniture factory but always by some irresistible, magnetic force she turned back to the obituary notices. She read them over two or three times. Yes, she had known them all.

She looked into the bright red and blue flames that burned in the fireplace. How many times had she gazed into that fireplace? How many cold winter mornings had she arisen from underneath her bright scrap quilts, hopped across the freezing floor and painfully built a fire there? Thousands of times! She had always lived in this house on the main residential street, and so had her father and his father before him. They had been real pioneers, she was proud of her heritage. But all that was past, her mother and father were dead, and her old friends were passing away, slowly, almost unobserved. No one would hardly think that it was the passing of a sort of dynasty, a dynasty of southern aristocracy—the hamlet, the village, the city. They were passing in the night, the tiny flames of their lives were being blown out by that strange and unseen force.

She pushed the paper out of her lap and closed her eyes. The heat and closeness of the room made her feel sleepy. She had almost fallen to sleep when she was awakened by the grandfather clock chiming the hour. One, two, three, four—

She looked up and she seemed a little startled, she sensed a presence in the room, other than her own. She reached for her glasses and, slipping them on, she looked about the room. Everything seemed in order. It was terribly quiet, there didn't even seem to be the sound of cars passing on the street.

When her eyes finally came to focus she saw him. He was standing directly in front of her. She gave a little gasp.

"Oh," she said, "it's you."

"You know me then?" said the young gentleman.

"Your face seems familiar." Her voice was calm and only surprised.

"I do not wonder," the gentleman spoke eloquently. "I know you quite well. I remember seeing you once when you were a very little girl, you were a sweet child. Don't you remember the time I came to visit your mother?"

Nannie looked at him hard. "No, I don't remember, you could not have known my mother—you are so young.

I am an old woman, my mother was dead before you were even born."

"Oh, no—no. I remember your mother quite well. A very reasonable woman. You look somewhat like her. The nose, the eyes, and you both had the same white hair. Quite remarkable, quite!" The man looked down at her. His eyes were very black and his lips were very red, almost as if he had them rouged. He seemed attractive to the old woman; she felt herself being drawn to him.

"I remember you now. Yes, of course, I was just a little girl. But I remember you, you came and woke me up very late one night, the night"—suddenly she gasped, a glint of recognition and horror swept her eyes—"the night my mother died!"

"That's right, my, but you have a remarkable memory, for one so old!" His voice inflected the last few words deliberately. "But you remember me many times since then. The night your father passed away, and there were countless other times. Yes, yes indeed, I have seen you many times and you me, it is only now, this moment, that you should have recognized me. Why, only the other night I was talking to an old friend of yours, Will Larson."

Nannie's face bleached white, her eyes were burning

from her head, she could not take her eyes from the man's face. She did not want him to touch her, just so long as he did not touch her she felt quite safe. Presently she said in a hollow voice:

"Then you must be—"

"Now come," interrupted the stranger. "My good lady, let us not quibble. It will not be bad, as a matter of fact it is a rather pleasant sensation."

She grasped the sides of the chair, and began to rock feverishly. "Get away," she whispered hoarsely. "Get away from me, don't touch me, no not now, is this all I am to get out of life, it isn't fair, stay away, please!"

"Oh," laughed the sleek young gentleman, "madam, you are behaving like a child about to take a castor oil. I assure you it is not the least bit unpleasant. Now, just come here, closer, closer, let me kiss you upon the brow, it will be quite painless, you feel so quiet and restful, it will be just like falling asleep."

Nannie pushed herself as far back in the chair as she could. His red painted lips were coming nearer. She wanted to scream but she couldn't even breathe. She hadn't ever thought it would be like this. She scrouged down in the lowest corners of the chair and pushed one of the pillows tightly over her face. He was strong, she could feel him pulling the pillow away from her. His face, his puckered lips, his amorous eyes; he was like some grotesque lover.

She heard a door slam. She screamed as loud as she could. "Beulah, Beulah, Beulah!" She heard the running footsteps. She pushed the pillow away. The colored woman's black face looked down at her.

"What's ailin' you, Miss Nannie? Is somthin' wrong? Do you want that I should call the doctah?"

"Where is he?"

"Whar is who, Miss Nannie? What you talkin' about?"

"He was here, I saw him, he was after me, oh, Beulah I tell you he was here."

"Aw, now, Miss Nannie, you been having those nightmares again."

Nannie's eyes lost their hysterical violet spark; she looked away from the troubled Beulah. The fire in the fireplace was dying slowly, the last flames dancing mincingly.

"Nightmare? This time? I wonder."

Louise

Ethel opened the door stealthily and looked up and down the dark corridor. It was deserted and she sighed with relief as she closed the door. Well, that was one thing done, and the only thing she had found out was that either Louise didn't keep her mail or she burned it. The rest of them must be down at dinner, she thought; I'll say I had a sick headache.

She crept down the stairs and went quickly across the great lounge, across the terrace, and into the dining room. The room was filled with the sound of girls' laughing and talking. Unobserved, she took her place next to Madame at the fourth table in the quietly pretentious dining salon of Miss Burke's Academy for Young Ladies.

In answer to Madame's questioning eyes, she lied, "I've been suffering from a severe headache—I lay down to rest and I suppose I must have fallen asleep—I did not hear the dinner chimes." She spoke with the smooth perfection of wording and accent that Miss Burke so desired all her students to acquire. Ethel was, in Miss Burke's opinion, the epitome of all that she could ever hope to attain among her students. A young lady of seventeen with background, wealth, and certainly a most brilliant mind. The majority of the Academy girls thought Ethel rather on the stupid side—that is, about life. Ethel, in turn, blamed her unpopularity upon Louise Semon, a French girl of exquisite beauty.

Louise was generally acknowledged to be the Queen Bee of the Academy. The girls worshipped her, and the teachers jealously admired her both for her mind and for her almost uncanny beauty. She was a tall girl, magnificently proportioned, with dark olive skin. Jet black hair framed her face and flowed rich and wavy to her shoulders—under certain lights it cast off a bluish halo. Her eyes, as Madame of table four had once exclaimed in a rapture of admiration, were as black as the night. She was dearly loved by everyone—everyone except Ethel and possibly Miss Burke herself, who somehow vaguely resented the girl's influence over the entire school. She did not feel that it was good for the school or for the girl herself. The girl had had excellent letters from the Petite Ecole in France and the Mantone Academy in Switzerland. Miss Burke had met neither of the girl's parents, who resided at their chalet in Geneva. All arrangements had been made through a Mr. Nicoll, Louise's American guardian, from whom Miss Burke received her check annually. Louise had come at the opening of the fall semester and had within five months put the Academy into the palm of her hand.

Ethel despised the Semon girl, who, it was rumored, was the daughter of a French Count and a Corsican heiress. She loathed everything about her—her looks, her popularity, the smallest detail of her person and mannerisms. And Ethel did not know exactly why—it was not altogether because she was jealous, though that was a great deal of it; it was not because she thought Louise laughed at her secretly or because she acted as if Ethel never existed—it was something else. Ethel suspected something about Louise that no one else would ever have dreamed of—and she meant to find out if she was right. Louise might not be so wonderful then. Maybe she hadn't found anything in her room this afternoon, not even a letter—nothing. But Ethel smiled across the dining room to the table where Louise sat gaily laughing and talking, the center of attention—for Ethel had a little interview planned with Miss Burke for that night!

II

The grandfather clock was chiming eight in the reception salon of Miss Burke's quarters where Ethel stood nervously waiting. The lights were dim, and the corners of the room were in darkness—the whole atmosphere was cold and Victorian. Ethel waited at the window—watching the first snowfall of the year, the white mantling of the naked trees and the dusty, silver cloaking of the earth. "I must write a poem about this sometime—'The First Snowfall' by Ethel Pendleton." She smiled wanly and sat down on a dark tapestried chair.

The door at the other end of the room opened and Mildred Barnett emerged from Miss Burke's private sitting room.

"Goodnight, Miss Burke, and thank you ever so much for your help."

Ethel moved away from the shadows and crossed the salon quickly. She paused at the door of Miss Burke's sitting room and took a deep breath; she knew just what she was going to say—after all, Miss Burke should know what she suspected; it was all for the good of the school, nothing else. But Ethel knew she was lying even to herself. She knocked softly and waited until she heard Miss Burke's high voice.

"Come in, please."

Miss Burke was seated in front of her fireplace, drinking a small China demi-tasse of coffee. There was no other light in the room and Ethel thought, as she sat down on the soft cushion at Miss Burke's feet, that it was strangely like a scene of peace and contentment on a holiday card.

"How nice of you to drop in on me, Ethel, my dear. Is there something that I may do for you?"

Ethel almost wanted to laugh—it was so funny, so ironic. In fifteen minutes this elderly, composed woman would be quite shaken.

"Miss Burke, something has come to my notice, which, I believe, warrants your immediate attention." She had chosen her language carefully and accented the words precisely in the manner that Miss Burke so heartily felt was correct and genteel. "It is in connection with Louise Semon. You see, a friend of my family's, a physician, called on me recently here at school and—"

Miss Burke put down her demi-tasse and listened to Ethel's story in shocked amazement. Her stately face flushed. Once during the recitation she exclaimed, "But, Ethel, this can not be true—I made all the arrangements through a person of obvious integrity—a Mr. Nicoll—surely he would know we could never allow such a thing—such a dreadful thing!"

"I know it is true," Ethel exclaimed, petulant at this disbelief; "I swear it! Call this Mr. Nicoll tomorrow, ask him—tell him the situation is intolerable and jeopardizing the standing of your school—if I am right. I know that I am. No—do not rely on Mr. Nicoll alone. Surely there are authorities—?"

And Miss Burke nodded. She was becoming more convinced and more shocked every minute. There was only the sound of Ethel's voice and the soft purr of the fire—and the gentle presence of falling snow, whispering at the window pane.

III

There was one pale light burning in the corridor when Ethel reached her room. The signal for lights out had been given a good hour before. She would have to undress in the dark. The instant she entered her room she knew something was wrong. She knew she was not alone.

In a frightened whisper, she said, "Who's here?" In sudden terror she thought, "It's Louise. Somehow she's found out—she knows—and she's come here."

Then, above the beating of her own heart, she heard the soft rustle of silk and a hand clutched her arm tightly.

"It is I—Mildred."

"Mildred Barnett?"

"Yes, I came here to stop what you're doing!"

Ethel attempted to laugh, but it stopped somewhere and she coughed instead. "I haven't the slightest—not even the foggiest notion what you're talking about. Stop what?" But she felt the falseness in her voice and she was frightened.

Mildred shook her. "You know what I mean! You saw Miss Burke tonight—I listened. Perhaps it's not the most honorable thing, but I'm glad I did if I can help Louise out of that lie you told tonight."

Ethel tried to push her accuser's arm away. "Stop it! you're hurting me!"

"You did lie—didn't you?" Mildred's voice was hoarse with fury.

"No—no—it was the truth—I swear it. Miss Burke's going to find out if it isn't the truth; then you'll see. You won't think little Miss Semon is so wonderful then!"

Mildred released her grip on Ethel. "Listen, it wouldn't make one particle of difference to me whether it was true or not—you aren't even in a class with that girl." She paused for a moment and chose her words carefully. "Take my advice—go to Miss Burke and tell her you were lying—or I'm not responsible for your health, Ethel Pendleton. You're playing with dynamite!"

With that as a farewell, she opened the door and slammed it with a bang.

Ethel stood shivering in the terrible darkness. It wasn't because of Louise—she didn't care about that—it was the others. Mildred would tell them probably, and that was why she suddenly knew she was going to cry.

IV

Miss Burke lay on the sofa of her sitting room, her head propped up by a huge pink silk pillow. Her hands were pushed tightly against her eyes, trying to drive away the dull ache which gnawed at her fraught nerves.

Miss Burke thought, with a shudder, of what would have happened if Ethel had told the other students instead of her, and they in turn had told their parents. Yes, Ethel should be congratulated.

When Ethel entered the headmistress's private kingdom, the clock in the reception salon was chiming five. The feeble winter sun had disappeared, and the gray January dusk filtered weakly through the heavily draped windows. She could see that Miss Burke was in an emotionally disturbed state.

"Good afternoon, dear." Miss Burke's voice was tired and strained.

"You wished to see me?" Ethel sought to keep herself, in appearance, as innocent as possible.

Miss Burke gestured with annoyance.

"Let us come to the point at once. You were correct. I called Mr. Nicoll and demanded a full report of the girl's parents. Her mother was an American negress, a mulatto to be exact, from the West. She was a sensational dancer in Paris and married a wealthy and titled Frenchman, Alexis Semon. So Louise is, as you suspected, a person of color. *Quadroon*, I believe, is the technical term. Most unfortunate. But naturally the situation is intolerable, as I explained to Mr. Nicoll. I told him she would receive immediate dismissal. He is calling for her tonight. Naturally, I had an interview with Louise and explained the situation to her as kindly as possible—oh, but why go into that?"

She looked at Ethel as if she were seeking sympathy—but all she saw was a young girl's face, whose thin lips were stretched in a sardonic smile of triumph. Miss Burke knew with sudden realization how she had played into this jealous girl's hands. Abruptly she said, "Will you please leave me."

When Ethel had gone, Miss Burke lay there on the sofa remembering, with horrible clarity, all the things Louise had said in her defense. What difference did it make? She did not look colored. She was as clever and as charming as any of the other girls—better educated than most. She was so happy here; was not America a democracy?

Miss Burke tried to soothe herself with the thought that what she had done had to be done—after all, hers was a fashionable institution. She had been tricked into accepting the girl. But something else kept telling her that she was wrong and that Louise was right!

V

It was nine o'clock and Ethel lay on her bed staring at the ceiling—trying not to think of anything or hear anything. She wanted to fall asleep and forget.

Suddenly there was a soft knock on the door. Then the door opened and Louise Semon was standing there.

Ethel shut her eyes tightly—she hadn't counted on this.

"What do you want?" She talked up to the ceiling and did not turn her head.

The beautiful girl stood by the bed and looked down directly into Ethel's face. Ethel could feel those dark eyes on her and she knew they were swollen from tears.

"I came to ask you why you did this to me. Do you dislike me so?"

"I hate you."

"Why?" Louise was earnest in asking.

"I don't know—please go; leave me alone!"

She could hear Louise opening the door. "Ethel, you are a strange girl. I am afraid I do not understand—" And the door was closed.

A few minutes later Ethel heard a car in the driveway. She went to the window and looked out. A black limousine was turning through the stone gates, out of the school grounds. When she turned around, Ethel was looking into the face of Mildred Barnett.

Mildred said simply, "Well, Ethel, you've won and you've lost, all at the same time. I told you you were playing with dynamite. Yes, Ethel, of a certain type you've given a rather brilliant performance—shall I applaud?"

This Is for Jamie

Almost every morning, except Sundays, Miss Julie took Teddy to play in the park. Teddy loved these daily trips. He would take along his bike or some plaything and amuse himself while Miss Julie, glad to be rid of him, gossiped with the other nurses and flirted with the officers. Teddy liked the park best in the morning when the sun was warm and the water spurted out of the fountains in a crystal spray.

"It looks just like gold, doesn't it, Miss Julie?" he would ask the white-garbed, carefully made-up nurse.

"I wish it were!" Miss Julie would grumble.

The night before the day Teddy met Jamie's mother it had rained, and in the morning the park was fresh and green. Although it was toward the end of September, it seemed more like a spring morning. Teddy ran along the paved paths of the park with a wild exuberance. He was an Indian, a detective, a robber-baron, a fairy-tale Prince, he was an angel, he was going to escape from the thieves through the bush—and most of all he was happy and he had two whole hours to himself.

He was playing with his cowboy rope when he saw her. She came along the path and sat down on one of the vacant benches. It was the dog she had with her that first attracted his attention. He loved dogs, he was crazy to have one, but Papa had said no, because he didn't want to have to housebreak a puppy and if you got a full-grown dog it wouldn't be the same. The woman's dog was just what he had always wanted. It was a wire haired terrier, hardly more than a puppy.

He walked slowly up, a little embarrassed, and patted the dog on the head.

"That's a fella," "Atta Boy." That's what they said in the movies and the adventure stories Miss Julie read him.

The woman looked up. Teddy thought she was about as old as his mother, but his mother didn't have such pretty hair. This was like gold and it was wavy and soft looking.

"He's an awfully nice dog. I wish I had one like him."

The woman smiled, and it was then that he thought she was very pretty. "He's not mine," she said. "He's my little boy's." Her voice was nice, too.

Immediately Teddy's eyes lit up. "Have you got a little boy like me?"

"Oh, he's a little bit older than you. He's nine."

Eagerly Teddy exclaimed, "I'm eight, or almost." He looked younger. He was small for his age and very dark. He was not a handsome child, but he had a friendly face and a disarming manner.

"What's your little boy's name?"

"Jamie—Jamie." She seemed happy, saying the name.

Teddy got up on the bench beside her. The dog was still in a playful mood and continued to jump on Teddy and scratch his legs.

"Sit down, Frisky," the woman commanded.

"Is that his name?" Teddy asked. "That's an awful cute name. He's such a nice dog. I wish I had a dog, and I could bring him to the park every day and we could play, and then at night he could sit in my room and I could talk to him instead of to Miss Julie, cause Frisky wouldn't care what I talked about—would'ja?"

The woman laughed a deep, somehow sad laugh. "I

guess maybe that's the reason Jamie's so crazy about Frisky."

Teddy cuddled the dog up against his leg.

"Does Jamie run with him in the park, and play Indians and things?"

The woman stopped smiling. She turned her gaze away toward the reservoir. For a moment he thought she was angry with him.

"No," she answered, "no, he doesn't run with Frisky. He just plays with him on the floor, he can't go outside. That's the reason I take Frisky for walks. Jamie's never been in the park—he's sick."

"Oh, I didn't know." Teddy's face flushed. Suddenly he saw Miss Julie coming up the path and he knew she would be angry if she saw him talking to a stranger.

"I hope I see you again," he said, "tell Jamie hello for me. I've got to go now, but maybe you'll be here tomorrow, huh?"

The woman smiled; he thought again how nice and pretty she was. He rushed down the path toward Miss Julie, who was feeding crumbs to the pigeons. He looked back and called, "Goodbye, Frisky," The woman's wavy hair shone in the sun.

II

That night he kept thinking of the woman and of the little boy, Jamie. He must be very sick if he couldn't go outside. And, while Teddy lay in bed, he saw Frisky over and over. He hoped that the woman would be there the next day.

In the morning Miss Julie awakened him with a shake and a sharp command. "Come on, you lazy bones! Get out of that bed this minute or you won't go to the park."

Immediately he jumped out of bed and ran to the window. It was clear and cool and with the fresh smell of early morning. It would be beautiful in the park today!

"Yippee, yippee," he yelled and ran wildly into the bathroom.

"Now what do you suppose has got into that child?" Miss Julie said, looking after the flashing Teddy in utter bewilderment.

When they reached the park, Teddy slipped away from Miss Julie while she stood talking with two other nursemaids. The long curving pathways of the park were almost deserted. He felt completely free and alone. He dodged through some underbrush and came out by the reservoir and there, just ahead of him, he saw the woman and the dog.

She looked up when the dog started to bark at Teddy.

"Hello, Teddy," she greeted him warmly.

He was pleased that she remembered him. How kind she was! "Hello, hello, Frisky." He sat down on the bench and the dog jumped on him, licking his hand and nudging against his ribs.

"Ouch," Teddy squealed. "That tickles."

"I've been waiting for you almost ten minutes," the woman said.

"Waiting for me?" he said, startled and sick with joy.

"Yes," she laughed. "I have to get back to Jamie sometime before the day's over."

"Yes," Teddy said hurriedly, happily. "Yes, you do, don't you? I'll bet he misses Frisky while he's out here in the park. I know I'd never let him out of my sight if he was mine."

"But Jamie isn't as lucky as you," she said. "He can't run and play."

Teddy fondled the dog; he pressed its cold nose to his warm cheek. He had heard that if their noses were cold, dogs were healthy.

"What's Jamie sick with?"

"Oh," she answered vaguely, "something like a cough, a bad cough."

"Then he can't be very sick," Teddy said brightly. "I've had plenty of coughs, and I've never stayed in bed more than two or three days."

She smiled a little. They sat in silence. Teddy cuddled the dog in his lap and wished he could jump up and run with him across the great green lawns marked "KEEP OFF THE GRASS."

Presently she got up and gathered the dog's leash in her hand. "I must go now," she said.

"You aren't leaving, are you?"

"Yes, I'm afraid I'll have to. I promised Jamie I'd be right back. I was just supposed to go down to the cigar store and get him some comic magazines. He'll be calling the police if I don't hurry up!"

"Oh," he said eagerly, "I have lots of comic magazines at home. I'll bring some tomorrow for Jamie!"

"Good," the woman said. "I'll tell him. He loves magazines." She started off down the path.

"I'll meet you here tomorrow and I'll bring the magazines. I'll bring lots of them!" he called after her.

"All right," she called back, "tomorrow." And as he stood watching her disappear he thought how wonderful it must be to have a mother like that and a dog like Frisky. Oh, Jamie was really such a lucky boy, he thought. Then he heard Miss Julie's sharp voice calling him.

"Teddy, Oh—yoo-hoo! Teddy come here this instant. Miss Julie's been looking everywhere for you. You are a naughty boy and Miss Julie's angry with you."

He turned laughing and ran toward her, and suddenly, running as fast as he could, he felt like a young sapling bending in the wind.

That night, after he had finished his supper and had had his bath, he set to work to gather up all his comic magazines. They were stuffed helter-skelter in his closet, cedar box, and bookshelf. Except for the brightly covered magazines, his bookshelf was a picture in solemn literature—*The Child's Book of Knowledge, The Child's Garden of Verse*, and *Books Every Child Should Know*.

He managed to gather thirty fairly recent issues together before his mother and father came to say good night. His mother was dressed in a long flowery evening gown and she had flowers and perfume in her hair. He loved the smell of gardenias, so pungently sweet. His father was in his tuxedo and carried his tall silk hat.

"What are all these magazines for?" his mother asked him.

"For a friend," said Teddy, hoping she wouldn't ask any more. It would not be quite as secretive, quite as exciting, if his mother knew about it.

"Come on, Ellen," his father said impatiently. "The curtain goes up at eight-thirty, and I'm tired of getting to shows right in the middle."

"Good night, darling!"

"Good night, Son."

He threw them a kiss as they closed the door behind them. Then, quickly, he turned back to his magazines. He got the sheet of wrapping paper his new suit had come in, and awkwardly wrapped them in it. It made a big package. He tied it up with thick, coarse string. Then he stepped back and looked at it. Something was wrong, he thought. It wasn't fancy enough; it didn't look like a gift.

He went to his desk, delved around inside and came up with a box of crayons. With alternating red and green letters, he printed, "THIS IS," then shifted to blue and red, "FOR JAMIE—FROM TEDDY."

Satisfied, he put the package away before Miss Julie came in to turn off his light and open the window.

The next morning before they started to the park, he got out his Red Sky Chief Wagon, put his package in and covered it with playthings.

When they reached the park, Teddy could tell it was going to be an easy matter to get away from Miss Julie. She had on her best dress. She was all excited and had on more lipstick than usual. Teddy knew that she was expecting to meet Officer O'Flaherty in the park. Officer O'Flaherty was Miss Julie's fiancée, at least as far as Miss Julie was concerned.

"Now, Teddy, you just run on and have a good time, but mind now, Miss Julie will meet you at the playground."

He ran as quickly as he could toward the reservoir. He couldn't take any short cuts with the wagon; it bumped along behind him.

He saw Frisky and the woman sitting on the bench.

"Well, here on time, I see," she laughed when she saw him.

He rolled the wagon up beside the bench, threw off his playthings and proudly exhibited his big parcel of magazines.

"Oh," she cried, "what a big package! Why, Jamie will never finish reading all these. He will love them, Teddy. Come here; let me kiss you."

He blushed slightly as she kissed him on his cheek.

"You're a sweet child," she said softly as she stood up

and gathered her coat about her. "We had to take Jamie to the hospital last night."

"Won't he be able to read the comics?" Teddy asked anxiously.

"Yes," she smiled, "yes, of course—it'll keep him busy. The only thing I'm worrying about is whether I'll be able to carry them all." She lifted the big package and sighed wearily. Frisky jumped around, pulling at the leash and almost making her drop them.

"Stop that, Frisky," Teddy cried.

"Well, thanks again, Teddy. I can't stay today." She waved her hand and started down the path. Frisky pulled back toward Teddy.

"Will you be here tomorrow?" Teddy called.

"I don't know—maybe," she called back; then she turned a bend and disappeared.

He wanted to run after her, to go with her to the hospital and see Jamie, and to play with Frisky and have the woman kiss him on the cheek again and tell him that he was a sweet child. Instead he went to the playground where he met Miss Julie and went home.

The next day he came to the park and went directly to the bench, but there was no one there. He waited for an hour and a half, and then, with a sudden sick knowledge, he knew that she wasn't coming—that she would never be back and that he would never see her again, nor Frisky. He wanted to cry, but he wouldn't let himself.

The next day was Sunday and he couldn't go to the park. In the morning he went to church. Then his grand-mother came to visit, and she mooned over him all afternoon.

"If you ask me, Ellen, that child's sick! He's been act-ing strange all afternoon. Why, I gave him money to go get a soda and he said he didn't want one. He said he wanted a dog, a wire haired dog that he could call Frisky. Now if that isn't the strangest thing!"

And that night his father tried to pry it out of him.

"Son, aren't you feeling well? You can tell me if there's anything wrong?"

Teddy pursed his small mouth. "Well, Papa, it's a dog, a little dog called Frisky—a sick boy's mother—Jamie—he—"

His mother came to the door. "Bill, if we're going to the Abbotts' you'd better hurry. They expect us for cock-tails at seven."

His father got up, looked at his watch and said, "I'll see you about this some other time, Son." Then he went out, and shortly afterward Teddy heard the apartment door slam.

He was lying stretched out across his bed crying when Miss Julie came in. She was very excited and her face was all flushed. She took him in her arms, and patted his head. It was the first time he had ever known her to comfort anyone. For a moment he almost liked her.

"Guess what, Teddy! Oh you just never will guess! Guess what?"

He looked up and stopped crying. "I don't want to guess. I don't feel like guessing. My mother and father don't love me—no one loves me—leastwise no one you know."

Miss Julie scoffed.

"Oh what a little ninnie you are, Teddy. Silly boy—oh well, I suppose we all go through this age."

Miss Julie and her ages!

"But you haven't guessed yet. Oh, well, I'll tell you. Mr. O'Flaherty has asked me to marry him!" Her face was wreathed in smile.

"Are you going to?" he asked.

She held out her hand and exhibited a silver ring with an amethyst stone, which Teddy took for an engagement ring.

Then she got up and hurried into her room. She did not come in to put him to bed that night nor to open the window.

The next morning he awoke very early. No one was up, not even Miss Julie, and no sound came from his parents' bed room, nor the maid's. Cautiously and quietly he dressed. Then he stole out of the apartment and down the long corridor toward the stairs. He did not dare ring for the elevator.

In the park it was chilly but beautiful. There was no one there except one man asleep on a bench. He was all huddled up and looked so cold and hungry and ugly that Teddy raced past him without daring to look a second time.

He went to the reservoir and sat down on the same old bench. He made up his mind he was going to sit there until Frisky and Jamie's mother came, even if it was all day.

The water was beautiful. He imagined it was some great ocean and he was sailing a ship across it, while musicians played in the background, just like at the movies.

He had been sitting a long while before he saw the first horseback rider. He knew it must be getting late if the riders were coming out. After that first one, they came thick and fast. He counted them as they passed. He had seen many celebrities riding in the park, but without

Miss Julie to identify them he could not tell them from ordinary people.

Then the carriages and nurses began to arrive. It was nearly ten o'clock. The sun had risen full and bright in the sky. In the drowsy warmth of its rays, he felt himself falling asleep.

Suddenly he heard a yelp and a bark. A little wire haired terrier jumped up on the bench beside him.

"Frisky—Frisky—" he cried. "It's you!"

A tall thin man was attached to the other end of the leash. Teddy gazed up at him bewilderedly.

"What's your name, Son?" the stranger asked.

"Teddy," he answered in a small, frightened voice.

The man handed him an envelope. "Then I guess this is for you."

Teddy tore it open anxiously. It was written in a long, graceful hand. He had a hard time reading it.

Dear Teddy,
Frisky is for you. Jamie would have wanted you to
have him.

It was unsigned. Teddy stared at it for a long time until he couldn't see it anymore. He grasped the dog to him and squeezed him as hard as he could. He could explain to Mama and Papa somehow.

Then he remembered the man. He looked up. He looked all around him but the man had gone and all he could see was the pathway and the trees and the grass and the reservoir gleaming in the morning sun.

Lucy

Lucy was really the outgrowth of my mother's love for southern cooking. I was spending the summer in the south when my mother wrote my aunt and asked her to find her a colored woman who could really cook and would be willing to come to New York.

After canvassing the territory, Lucy was the result. Her skin was a rich olive and her features were finer and lighter than most negroes'. She was tall and reasonably round. She had been one of the teachers at the school for colored children. But she seemed to have a natural intelligence, not formed by books, but a child of the earth with a deep understanding and compassion for all that lived. As most southern negroes, she was very religious, and even now, I can see her sitting in the kitchen reading her Bible, and declaring most earnestly to me that she was a "child of God."

So we had Lucy, and when she stepped off the train that September morning at Pennsylvania Station, you could see the pride and the triumph in her eyes. She told me that all her life she had wanted to come north, and, as she put it, "to live like a human being." That morning she felt that she would never want again to see Jim Crow with all its bigotry and cruelty.

At that time we lived in an apartment on Riverside Drive. From all of the front windows we had an excellent view of the Hudson River and the Jersey Palisades, rising steep against the sky. In the morning they looked like heralds greeting the dawn and in the evening, at sunset, when the water was dyed in the confusion of crimson shades, the cliffs shone magnificently, like sentinels of an ancient world.

Sometimes, at sunset, Lucy would sit at the apartment window and gaze lovingly at the spectacle of the dying day in the world's greatest metropolis.

"Um, um," she would declare, "if only Mama and George were here to see this." And at first she loved the bright lights and all the noise. Almost every Saturday she took me down to Broadway and we went on theatrical sprees. She was crazy about the vaudevilles, and the Wrigley sign was a show in itself.

Lucy and I were constant companions. Sometimes in the afternoon after school she would help me with my mathematical homework, she was very adroit at mathematics. She read a great deal of poetry, but she didn't know anything about it except that she loved the sound of the words, and occasionally the sentiment behind them. It was through these readings that I first became aware of how homesick she really was. When she read poems with a southern theme, she read them beautifully, with a unique compassion. Her soft voice recited the lines tenderly, understandingly, and if I glanced up quickly enough there was just the trace of a tear gleaming in the exquisite blackness of those negro eyes. Then she would laugh if I mentioned it and shrug her shoulders.

"It was pretty though, wasn't it?"

When Lucy worked she invariably accompanied her actions with a soft singing, "blues" in its quality. I liked to hear her sing. Once we went to see Ethel Waters and she went around the house imitating Ethel for days, then finally she announced she was going to enter an amateur contest. I'll never forget that contest. Lucy won second place, and my hands were raw from applauding. She sang "It's De-Lovely, It's Delicious, It's Delightful." I remember the words even now, we rehearsed them so many times. She was scared to death she was going to forget them and when she went on the stage, her voice tremored just enough to give it a Ethel Waterish tone.

But eventually Lucy abandoned her musical career, because she met Pedro, and she didn't have time for much else. He was one of the basement workers in the building and he and Lucy were thicker than molasses. Lucy had been in New York only five months when this happened and she was still, technically speaking, green. Pedro was very slick, he dressed flashy, and besides I was mad because I didn't get to go to the shows anymore. Mama laughed and said, "Well, I guess we've lost her, she'll go northern too." She didn't seem to care so much, but I did.

Finally, Lucy didn't like Pedro either, and then she was more lonesome than ever. Sometimes I would read her mail when it was lying around open. It went something like this,

Dear Lucy,

Yu Pa he's got sick, he in bed now. He say, hallo.
We guess now yo up thea yo hev no time fo us po

folk. Yo brother, George, he done gone to Pensacola,
he work in bottle factry thea. We sends you all
ouah love,

Mama

Sometimes, late at night, I could hear her softly crying in her room, and then I knew she was going home.
New York was just vast loneliness. The Hudson River
kept whispering "Alabama River." Yes, Alabama River
with all its red muddy water flowing high to the bank and
with all its swampy little tributaries.

All the bright lights—a few lanterns shining in the
darkness, the lonely sound of a whip-poor-will, a train
screaming its haunting cry in the night. Hard cement,
bright cold steel, smoke, burlesque, the smothered sound
of the subway in the dank, underground tube. Rattle,
Rattle,—soft green grass—and yes sun, hot, plenty hot,
but so soothing, bare feet, and cool, sand-bedded stream
with soft round pebbles smooth, like soap. The city, no
place for one of the earth, Mama's calling me home.
George, I'm God's child.

Yes, I knew she was going back. So when she told me
she was leaving I wasn't surprised. I opened and shut my

mouth and felt the tears in my eyes and the empty feeling in my stomach.

It was in May that she left. It was a warm night and the sky over the city was red in the night. I gave her a box of candy, all chocolate-covered cherries (because that was what she liked best), and a pack of magazines.

Mother and Daddy drove her to the bus station. When they left the apartment I ran to my window and leaned over the sill until I saw them come out and climb into the car, and slowly, gracefully glide out of view.

Already I could hear her saying, "Ohhhh, Mama, New York's wonderful, all the people, and I saw movie stars in person, oh, Mama!"

Traffic West

IV

Four chairs and a table. On the table, paper—in the chairs, men. Windows above the street. On the street, people—against the windows, rain. This were, perhaps, an abstraction, a painted picture only, but that the people, innocent, unsuspecting, moved below, and the rain fell wet on the window.

For the men stirred not, the legal, precise document, on the table moved not. Then—

"Gentlemen, our four interests have been brought together, checked, and harmonized. Each one's actions now should to his own particulars be bent. And so I make a suggestion that we signify consent, attach our names hereto, and part."

A man rose, a paper in his hands. Another rose. He took the paper, scanned, and spoke.

"This satisfies our needs; we drew it well. Indeed, our companies are by this piece assured advantage and security. Yes, in this document I read great profit. I'll sign."

A third arose. He fixed his lens, perused the scroll. His lips in silence moved, and when words sounded, each was weighed.

"We must admit—our lawyers, too, agree—the text and wording of this note *is clear*. I have it from advice on every hand: herein is, despite the power it assumes, what legally can be, what by the law is. Thus, I'll sign." He read the script anew, and passed it to the fourth.

An executive like the others, he fain would have affixed his name and gone. But his brow clouded. He sat, reading, scanning, examining. Then he laid the paper down.

"I cannot, though agreeing, sign the document. Nor can you." He saw their startled faces. "It is the power of the thing that damns it. The very reasons you have just given, that show the lawful measures it *allows*. The purposes of *huge* extent, the full *assurance* of support, the mighty steps *permitted* these things, though lawful, are not for us. If unlawful, we could risk it, for the law would then be acting contrary—*supporting*, not oppressing, the thousands of workers; protecting, not destroying, the interests of weaker peoples.

"But if the law, our government, allows we *have* the right to make this tract to move, through legal pen, ten thousands for what our interests want—and worse, to misuse those same ones whose rights we represent; then *we* must draw the line—reject a measure which risks the welfare of the many in our care.

"We have power, as do all who serve great interests. But if we judge by God, a thing most difficult for mon-eyed minds to do, we sense, as men of might, our duty to the 'average man,' and, gentlemen, I beg you, take no such selfish action."

Again the room was still. A businessman had just torn down one kind of code, and in this tearing down revealed another.

Three others saw his reasoning, and, having seen, re-placed old business goals with goals of brotherhood.

"Let us take the bus away from here, and leave the document destroyed in legal fashion."

III

The bright morning sun streaked over rows of waiting roofs and struck against the closely drawn blinds of the house on the hill.

The covers on a huge, medieval bed stirred and a sleepy head turned on the pillow as a knock sounded on the door.

Two freshly shaven, trim young men filed into the room.

"Good morning, Uncle. Your orange juice," greeted one as his brother stepped to the windows and raised the blinds. The eager sun thus welcomed streamed into the room.

"You're late, Gregory," growled the man in bed. He sipped his juice, then raised himself. "And damn it! If Minnie leaves seeds in this drink once more, I'll get rid of her." He spat the seed on the rug.

"Pick it up, Henry, and throw it in the wastebasket," he commanded.

"Uncle," grinned Gregory as he returned from the receptacle. "How's your leg? We've good news—"

"Shut up," the older man rasped. "When I tell Henry to do something, I want *Henry* to do it. You may be twins but I can tell you apart. So, Gregory, pick that seed out of the wastebasket and let Henry do as I said.

"All my life I've seen to it that things were *just so*. I've kept my library exactly the same way. I've kept my room exactly the same way. I've kept the house the same way. I've gone to town and worked. I've gone to church and prayed—exactly the same way. I've thought and acted as I should have. My great strength as mayor has not been in myself but in my sound habits—"

"Oh, you'll be elected again, Uncle," cheered one. "But right now, we've good news for you—"

"Hell, boy, of course I'll be elected!" interrupted the invalid. "I'm not talking about that. He signaled impatiently for an extra pillow. "My greatest worry is you two. Your dead father wanted me to take care of you. But God, what can I do? I break my leg—it'll have to come off, you know. I send for you two to be in my office until I recover. Hell! It's one thing to lose a leg, but it's too much to lose an election because of someone else's stupidity. And, say, did you touch that cross word puzzle on the floor? . . . Good, I've got to have some relaxation."

"We've good, news, Uncle—"

But he had sunk back in his covers. His rage was

abating. He noticed sunshine playing on the top of his bed. "Listen to me first." His voice was sad.

"I've lived a good life." He turned to them. "But I've never had any fun. Not a bit. Being too busy to marry. I've left women quite alone. I didn't smoke, or drink, or sw— Hell. I could swear, but *it's* no fun. And I never enjoyed golf, couldn't break ninety. Never liked music, either—or poetry, or—" He thought of his cross word puzzle. He became silent, remained silent. . . . His mind followed a strange course, one it had never taken before.

The sun was saying "hello" to his face now.

"By Jove, boys!" he cried, "I've never looked at it that way! Politics is one big cross word puzzle—delightful. And"—he sat bolt upright—"so is life! Aaaaaaa!" He had never smiled like this. "Last night, Henry, I thought I might make something of myself, if I only had two legs. But now, lame or *not,* I see I can be just like—just like"—he glanced around the room—"Yes! just like the sun!"

He pointed a trembling, happy finger at the ball of fire.

"*Our* uncle!" laughed the twins, and Henry said, "Your legs are your own. That is the good news! The doctor has declared the amputation unnecessary. You should begin walking as soon as possible. Tomorrow afternoon the three of us will take the bus to town!"

II

A ten-inch record whirled on the turntable. From a small speaker issued a beautiful, stirring trumpet solo. The girl rose from the bench on which she had been seated. She reached for the switch and the high trumpet tones died away in a gurgling gasp.

The music had disturbed her; she was dreaming of her childhood.

Outside the little try-out room, row upon row of record albums hemmed in two men. One pulled out a Beethoven quartet and handed it to the other.

"You can try this out, sir, as soon as the young woman is through with the machine."

"No need," laughed the other. "I think I can trust the Budapest String Quartet without hearing them." The girl appeared from the booth and laid fifty-five cents on the counter.

"I'll take it," she said, holding up the disc. And so, man and girl left the Music Shop, records under their arms.

"It's a warm day," she began.

"Oh," he replied, "the day holds nothing for me. Nor does the night anymore."

"Do you feel that way, too?" she returned quickly. "Do you feel that—that you're like an engine on a track— just going you don't know where?" She turned red—he was a stranger after all. "But I'm serious, do you see any point in living?"

"I have no night; I have no day," he replied sincerely. "I really have only one thing." He held up his album. "My very life hangs on music." He turned to the girl. He saw that she *was* pretty, but it was more her charm than her face. With a friendly motion, he put his hand in hers. "Are you going through the park?"

"I can," she replied, and they stepped along the pathway. A minute later they came upon a wooden bench between two trees.

"I always stop here for a spell," he said, loosening her hand. "Perhaps we'll meet again."

The color mounted on her cheeks. She trembled slightly and, touching his coat with one hand, whispered. "Do you mind if I sit with you? Oh *please*! I must!" She stood silent.

He bit his lips, gently took her record, and, placing it on the bench with his album, pulled her down beside him. A moment later he drew her closer, then, slowly, placed one arm behind her.

"I was afraid to hope it," he murmured, "for from the moment I first saw you, I knew why music meant so much to me. It was sort of a substitute—a glorious substitute, for something finer—for something—something"—he looked at her—"like you."

They sat there, each thrilled by the other.

"The earth spins round us now like one huge record," he went on. "This record plays—hear, listen, see—it is the song of life!

"Now, music is everywhere. These trees, this grass, this sky, swing to our rhythm." He stretched out one arm. "Oh love!" He bent down and kissed her.

"Tomorrow afternoon we'll take the bus, and go to town for a license, and the rest."

"Yes," she sang, fixing his collar.

I

Dear Mother,

I write this note, dear Mother, with truly humbled pen. I see beyond my weaknesses and those of fellow men. Yet only as the sun rose up this morning.

My first ten years of life I filled with self, self, self, and self alone. Only cared I for the things you gave me. I wanted food, sleep, and pleasure. I was as a monkey self-intent. I cared not who was near me nor cared why.

And then, the next few years instilled in me a growing sense of "presence." Presence of what cared I not, but only knew that if I did a right, this "presence" smiled. But when on self I thought— and, so thinking, wronged another—this "presence" scowled.

At length I grew to love this "presence" and to call it God. It helped me see it was the truth of life. I saw it should be followed and I tried to draw it near. But it said, "You are not ready," and hovered near.

I was discouraged when I found I had it not. I flatly told it off, returned—almost to the first stage of my life. I took up smoking, swore, had a good time—thought I didn't care.

But then this "presence" whispered encouragements to me. I listened. It held before me such a light, I couldn't help but try. I only feared this light I might not reach before I die.

In struggling, I found my frailty. And God, in whisperings, showed me, too, my strengths. And so I did discover another method: failing that, a personal creed to cover both talents and setbacks was necessary.

Indeed, it did great wonders, for the difficulty of fulfillment gave me a chance to know and try my strength.

Yet found I that this creed could not be filled, and so I added to it "Presence of God," which made, with sure conviction, all pain and inconveniences worthwhile.

Even with this addition, would the light not come. I now was struggling only for HIS PRESENCE within me; yet, I had it not. I let Him talk to me; I begged Him to. I followed what He would: His will, I tried to do.

And so, the sun bore a gift for me today. Dear Mother, "it" has come to me—and on the perfect day. The perfect day, because in my hand I hold acceptance to the Armed Forces of the United States of America. I'll take the bus tomorrow.

Your loving son _____

O

Associated Press—"Ten people were killed tonight in the worst traffic disaster of the season. A late afternoon bus collided with an oncoming truck and overturned. The dead included four business executives, the mayor of a small town, and a young woman. For a complete list of the deceased, turn to page thirty-two."

"For every man must get to heaven his own way."

Kindred Spirits

"Of course, it did give me rather a turn; he fell an enormous distance from over the bridge railing to the river: made scarcely a splash. And there was absolutely no one in sight." Mrs. Martin Rittenhouse paused to sigh and stir her tea. "I was wearing a blue dress when it happened. Such a lovely dress—matched my eyes. Poor Martin was very fond of it."

"But I understand drowning is pleasant," said Mrs. Green.

"Oh, yes indeed: an extremely pleasant method of— of departure. Yes, I think if the poor man could have chosen his own way out, I'm certain he would have preferred—water. But, harsh as it may sound, I can't pretend I wasn't considerably cheered to be rid of him."

"So?"

"Drank, among other things," confided Mrs. Ritten-house grimly. "He was also somewhat over-affectionate, inclined to—dally. And prevaricate."

"Lie, you mean?"

"Among other things."

It was a narrow, high-ceilinged room in which the two ladies talked: a comfortable setting, but without any spe-cial distinction. Faded green draperies were drawn against a winter afternoon; a fire, purring drowsily in a stone fire-place, reflected yellow pools in the eyes of a cat, limply curled beside the hearth; a cluster of bells, wound round the throat of the cat, pealed icily whenever he stirred.

"I've never liked men named Martin," said Mrs. Green.

Mrs. Rittenhouse, the visitor, nodded. She was perched stiffly in a fragile-looking chair, persistently churning her tea with a lemon slice. She wore a deep purple dress, and a black, shovel-shaped hat over curly, wig-like grey hair. Her face was thin, but constructed along stern lines, as though modeled by rigorous disci-pline: a face which seemed content with a single, stricken expression.

"Nor men named Harry," added Mrs. Green, whose husband's name was precisely that. Mrs. Green and her two hundred odd pounds (concealed in a flesh-colored negligee) luxuriously consumed the major portion of a three-seat couch. Her face was huge and hearty, and her eyebrows, plucked nearly naked, were penciled in such an absurd manner that she looked as if someone had startled her in the midst of a shamefully private act. She was filing her nails.

Now between these two women was a connection difficult to define: not friendship, but something more. Perhaps Mrs. Rittenhouse came closest to putting a finger on it when once she said, "We are kindred spirits."

"This all happened in Italy?"

"France," corrected Mrs. Rittenhouse. "Marseille, to be exact. Marvelous city—subtle—all lights and shadows. While Martin fell, I could hear him screaming: quite sinister. Yes, Marseille was exciting. He couldn't swim a stroke, poor man."

Mrs. Green hid the fingernail file between the couch cushions. "Personally, I feel no pity," she said. "Had it been I—well, he might have had a little help getting over that rail."

"Really?" said Mrs. Rittenhouse, her expression brightening slightly.

"Of course. I've never liked the sound of him. Remember what you told me about the incident in Venice?

Aside from that, he manufactured sausage or something, didn't he?"

Mrs. Rittenhouse made a sour bud of her lips. "He was the sausage king. At least, that is what he always claimed. But I shouldn't complain: the company sold for a fabulous sum, although it's beyond me why anyone would want to eat a sausage."

"And look at you!" trumpeted Mrs. Green, waving a well-nourished hand. "Look at you—a free woman. Free to buy and do whatever you please. While I—" she laced her fingers together and solemnly shook her head. "Another cup of tea?"

"Thank you. One lump, please."

Sparks whirred as a log crumpled in the fire. An ormolu clock, set atop the mantel, tolled the time with musical shafts of sound that played on the quiet: five.

Presently, Mrs. Rittenhouse, in a voice sad with memory, said, "I gave the blue dress to a chambermaid at our hotel: there was a tear in the collar where he clutched at me before he fell. And then I went to Paris and lived in a beautiful apartment till Spring. It was a lovely Spring: the children in the park were so neat and quiet; I sat all day feeding crumbs to the pigeons. Parisians are neurotic."

"Was the funeral expensive? Martin's, I mean?"

Mrs. Rittenhouse chuckled gently and, leaning forward, whispered, "I had him cremated. Isn't that priceless? Oh, yes—just wrapped the ashes in a shoebox and sent them to Egypt. Why there, I don't know. Except that he loathed Egypt. I loved it, myself. Marvelous country, but he never wanted to go. That's why it's priceless. However, there is this one thing I find extremely reassuring: I wrote a return address on the package and *it never came back*. Somehow I feel he must have reached his proper resting place, after all."

Mrs. Green slapped her thigh and bellowed, "The Sausage King among the Pharaohs!" And Mrs. Rittenhouse enjoyed the jest as much as her natural inscrutability would permit.

"But Egypt," sighed Mrs. Green, brushing tears of laughter from her eyes. "I always say to myself—'Hilda, you were intended for a life of travel—India, the Orient, Hawaii.' That's what I always say to myself." And then, with some disgust, she added, "But you've never met Harry, have you? Oh, my God! Hopelessly dull. Hopelessly bourgeois. Hopelessly!"

"I know the breed," said Mrs. Rittenhouse acidly. "Call themselves the backbone of the nation. Ha, not even nuisance value. My dear, it comes down to this: If they haven't money—get rid of them. If they have—who could make better use of it than oneself?"

"How right you are!"

"Well, it's pathetic and useless to waste yourself on that sort of man. Or any man."

"Precisely," was Mrs. Green's comment. She shifted position, her huge body quivering under the negligee, and dimpled her beefy cheek with a thoughtful finger. "I've often considered divorcing Harry," she said. "But that's very, very expensive. Then, too, we've been married nineteen years (and engaged five before that) and if I were to even suggest such a thing, I'm positive the shock would just about—"

"Kill him," ended Mrs. Rittenhouse, quickly lowering her eyes to the tea-cup. A flush of color kindled her cheeks and her lips pursed and unpursed with alarming rapidity. After a little, she said, "I've been thinking of a trip to Mexico. There's a charming place on the coast called Acapulco. A great many artists live there: they paint the sea by moonlight—"

"Mexico. Me-hi-co," said Mrs. Green. "The name sings. Ac-a-pul-co, Me-hi-co." She slammed her palm on the couch's arm. "God, what I wouldn't give to go with you."

"Why not?"

"Why not! Oh, I can just hear Harry saying, 'Sure, how much will you need?' Oh, I can just hear it!" She pounded the couch-arm again. "Naturally, if I had money of my own—well, I haven't, so that's that."

Mrs. Rittenhouse turned a speculative eye towards the ceiling; when she spoke her lips barely moved. "But Henry does, doesn't he?"

"A little—his insurance—eight thousand or so in the bank—that's all," replied Mrs. Green, and there was nothing casual in her tone.

"It would be ideal," said Mrs. Rittenhouse, pressing a thin, crepey hand on the other woman's knee. "Ideal. Just us two. We will rent a little stone house in the mountains overlooking the sea. And in the patio (for we shall have a patio) there will be fruit trees and jasmine, and on certain evenings we shall string Japanese lanterns and have parties for all the artists—"

"Lovely!"

"—and employ a guitarist to serenade. It shall all be one splendid succession of sunsets and starlight and enchanting walks by the sea."

For a long time their eyes exchanged a curious, searching gaze; and the mysterious understanding between them flowered into a mutual smile, which, in Mrs. Green's case, developed to a giggle. "That's silly," she said. "I could never do a thing like that. I would be afraid of getting caught."

"From Paris I went to London," said Mrs. Rittenhouse, withdrawing her hand and tilting her head at a severe angle; yet her disappointment could not be disguised. "A depressing place: dreadfully hot in the summer. A friend of mine introduced me to the Prime Minister. He was—"

"Poison?"

"—a charming person."

The bells tinkled as the cat stretched and bathed his paws. Shadow-like, he paraded across the room, his tail arched in the air like a feathered wand; to and fro he stroked his sides against his mistress's stupendous leg. She lifted him, held him to her bosom, and planted a noisy kiss on his nose; "Mummy's angel."

"Germs," declared Mrs. Rittenhouse.

The cat arranged himself languidly and fixed an impertinent stare upon Mrs. Rittenhouse. "I've heard of untraceable poisons, but it's all vague and story-bookish," said Mrs. Green.

"Never poison. Too dangerous, too easily detected."

"But let us *suppose* that we were going to—to rid ourselves of someone. How would you begin?"

Mrs. Rittenhouse closed her eyes and traced her finger round the rim of the tea-cup. Several words stuttered on her lips, but she said nothing.

"Pistol?"

"No. Definitely no. Firearms involve all sorts of whatnot. At any rate, I don't believe insurance companies recognize suicide—that is what it would have to appear to be. No, accidents are best."

"But the Good Lord would have to take credit for that."

"Not necessarily."

Mrs. Green, plucking at a stray wisp of hair, said, "Oh, stop teasing and talking riddles: what's the answer?"

"I'm afraid there is no consistently true one," said Mrs. Rittenhouse. "It depends as much upon the setting as the situation. Now, if this were a foreign country it would be simpler. The Marseille police, for instance, took very casual interest in Martin's accident: their investigation was most unthorough."

A look of mild surprise illumined Mrs. Green's face. "I see," she said slowly. "But then, this is *not* Marseille."

And presently volunteered, "Harry swims like a fish: he won a cup at Yale."

"However," continued Mrs. Rittenhouse, "it is by no means impossible. Let me tell you of a statement I read recently in the *Tribune*: 'Each year a larger percentage of deaths are caused by people falling in their bathtub than by all other accidents combined.'" She paused and eyed Mrs. Green intently. "I find that quite provocative, don't you?"

"I'm not sure whether I follow—"

A brittle smile toyed with the corners of Mrs. Rittenhouse's mouth; her hands moved together, the tips of her fingers delicately meeting and forming a crisp, blue-veined steeple. "Well," she began, "let us suppose that upon the evening the—tragedy—is scheduled, something apparently goes wrong with, say, a bathroom faucet. What does one do?"

"What *does* one do?" echoed Mrs. Green, frowning.

"This: call to him and ask if he would mind stepping in there a moment. You point to the faucet and then, as he bends to investigate, strike the base of his head—*right back here, see?*—with something good and heavy. Simplicity itself."

But Mrs. Green's frown persisted. "Honestly, I don't see where that is any accident."

"If you're determined to be so literal!"

"But I don't see—"

"Hush," said Mrs. Rittenhouse, "and listen. Now, this is what one would do next: undress him, fill the tub brim full, drop in a cake of soap and submerge—the corpse." Her smile returned and curved to a wider crescent. "What is the obvious conclusion?"

Mrs. Green's interest was complete, and her eyes were very wide. "What?" she breathed.

"He slipped on the soap, hit his head—and drowned."

The clock tuned six; the notes shimmered away in silence. The fire had gradually sifted to a slumbering bed of coals, and a chill seemed settled on the room like a net spun of ice. The cat's bells shattered the mood as Mrs. Green dropped him plumply to the floor, rose and walked to the window. She parted the draperies and looked out; the sky was drained of color; it was starting to rain: the first drops beaded the glass, distorting an eerie reflection of Mrs. Rittenhouse to which Mrs. Green addressed her next remark:

"Poor man."

Where the World Begins

Miss Carter had been explaining the eccentricities of Algebra for almost twenty minutes now. Sally looked disgustedly up at the snail-like hands of the school-room clock, only twenty-five more minutes and then freedom—sweet, precious freedom.

She looked at the piece of yellow paper in front of her for the hundredth time. Empty. Ah, well! Sally glanced around her, staring with contempt at the hard working mathematical students. "Humnph," she thought, "as if they're goin' to make a success in life just by addin' up a lot of figures, an' X's that don't make any sense anyway. Humnph, wait'll they get out in the world."

Exactly what getting out in the world or life was, she wasn't sure; however, her elders had led her to believe it was some horrible ordeal that she was going to have to undergo at some definite, future date.

"Uh, oh," she moaned, "here comes Robot." She called Miss Carter "Robot," because that was what Miss Carter reminded her of, a perfect machine, accurate, well oiled and as cold and shiny as steel. Hurriedly she scribbled a mass of illegible numbers over the yellow paper. "At least," Sally thought, "that'll make her think I'm working."

Miss Carter sailed past her without even a look. Sally breathed a deep sigh of relief. Robot!

Her seat was right next to the window. The room was on the third floor of the High School and from where she sat she could see a beautiful view. She turned to gaze outside. Her eyes became dilated, and glassy and unseeing—

"This year it makes us very happy to present the Academy Award for the finest portrayal of the year to Miss Sally Lamb for her unparalleled performance in *Desire*. Miss Lamb, you will please accept Oscar on behalf of myself and my associates."

A beautiful, striking woman reaches out and gathers the gold statuette in her arms.

"Thank you," she says in a deep, rich voice. "I suppose when something wonderful like this happens to anyone they're supposed to make a speech, but I'm just too grateful to say anything."

And then she sits down with the applause ringing in her ears. Bravo for Miss Lamb. Hurray. Clap, clap, clap, clap. Champagne. Did you really like me? Autograph? But certainly— What did you say your first name was, dear boy—John? Oh, French, Jean— All right— "To Jean, a dear friend, Sally Lamb." Autograph, please, Miss Lamb, autograph, autograph—Star, money, fame, beautiful, glamorous—Clark Gable—

"Are you listening, Sally?" Miss Carter sounded very angry. Sally jumped around, startled. "Yes, ma'am."

"Well, then, if you're paying such undivided attention perhaps you can explain this last problem I put on the board." Miss Carter's gaze swept the class superciliously.

Sally stared helplessly at the board. She could feel Robot's cold eyes on her and the giggling brats. She could have choked them all until their tongues hung out. Damn them. Oh, well, she was licked, the numbers, the squares, the crazy X's, Greek!

"Just as I thought," the Robot announced triumphantly. "Yes, just as I thought! You've been off in space again. I would like to know what goes on in that head of yours—certainly it has nothing to do with your school work. For a girl who's so—so, stupid, it looks like you could at least favor us with your attention. It's not just you, Sally, but you disrupt the whole class."

Sally hung her head and drew crazy little designs all over the paper. She knew her face was cerise, but she wasn't going to be like these other stupid morons who giggled and carried on every time the teacher bawled them out—even old Robot.

GOSSIP COLUMN:
What number one debutante of the season whose initials are Sally Lamb was seen romancing at the Stork Club with millionaire playboy Stevie Swift?

"Oh, Marie, Marie," called the beautiful young girl lying on the huge silken bed. "Bring me the new *Life* magazine."

"Yes, Miss Lamb," answered the prim French maid.

"Hurry, please," called the impatient heiress. "I want to see if that photographer did me justice; my picture's on the cover this week, you know. Oh, and while you're about it bring me an Alka-Seltzer—dastardly head-ache, too much champagne I guess."

RADIO:

Rich girl makes Debut Tonight. The long awaited Social Event of the Season brings forth Sally Lamb to Society in a brilliant Ten thousand dollar Ball. Nice work if you can get it! Flash, flash—

"Will you please pass your papers to the front of the room, hurry it up, please!" Miss Carter rapped her fingers impatiently against her desk.

Sally shoved her illegible paper over the shoulder of the pink faced boy that sat in front of her. Children. Humnph. She pulled her big Scottish plaid handbook over to her, delved around inside, and came up with a compact, lipstick, comb, and Kleenex.

She gazed at herself in the powder-dusty mirror as she smeared the lipstick on her pretty shaped lips. Raspberry.

The tall, slinky woman stood admiring her image in front of a huge gilt mirror at one of the more spectacular residences in Germany. She patted a stray hair back into her elaborate silver coiffure.

A dark, handsome gentleman bent over and kissed her bare shoulder. She smiled faintly.

"Ah, Lupé, how lovely you look tonight. You are so beautiful, Lupé. Your skin, so white, your eyes—Ach . . . you can't imagine what they make me feel."

"Umm," purred the Lady, "that, General, is where you are mistaken." She reached over to a marble table and picked up two wine glasses, slipped three pills into one, and handed it to the General.

"Lupé, I must see you more often. We will dine together every night when I return from the front."

"Ohhh, does my little baby have to go up there where all the fighting is?" Her raspberry lips were close to his. How clever you are, Sally, she thought.

"Lupé knows I have to carry the army maneuver plans up to the front, doesn't Lupé?"

"Do you have the plans with you?" queried the charming fifth columnist.

"Why, yes, but of course." She could see that he was passing out, his eyes were getting glassy and he looked very drunk. By the time the Mata Hari had finished her 1928 vintage, the General was stretched out at her feet.

She stooped down and began searching his coat.

Suddenly she heard boot steps outside—her heart jumped—

The bell went off with a loud clang. The students rushed helter-skelter for the door way. Sally put her make-up articles back in her handbag, gathered up her books, and prepared to depart.

"Just a minute, Sally Lamb," Miss Carter called her back. Robot again. "Come back here a minute—I want to talk to you."

By the time she reached the desk Miss Carter had finished filling out a form and handed it to her.

"That is a detention hall slip, you will go to detention hall this afternoon until it is over. I have told you numerously that I do not want you primping yourself in class. Do you want us to all get your germs?"

Sally blushed. She resented any reference to her anatomy or pertaining there of.

"And another thing, young lady, you didn't hand in your homework . . . Well, as I've told you, it's up to you whether you want to do your work or not . . . It's certainly not any skin off my back—"

Sally wondered vaguely whether she had any skin on her back—or was it tin?

"—you know, of course, that you're failing this subject. It's a mystery to me how anyone could so completely waste their time—I do not understand it—not at all. I think it would be better if you dropped this course, because, to be quite candid, I don't believe that you are mentally capable of doing the work. I—I—wait a minute—where do you think—"

Sally had thrown her books down on the desk and run out of the room. She knew she was going to cry and she didn't want to—not in front of Robot.

Damn her anyhow! What does she know about life. She doesn't know anything but a lot of numbers—Damn her anyway!

She worked her way on down the crowded halls.

The torpedo had hit about a half an hour ago and the ship was sinking fast. This was a chance! Sally Lamb, America's foremost newspaper woman, right here on the spot. She had gotten her camera out of her water logged cabin. And here she was, snapping pictures of the refugees climbing into the lifeboats and of her fellow sufferers struggling in the raging sea.

"Hey, Miss," called one of the sailors. "Yuh, better take this lifeboat, I think it's the last one."

"No thanks," she called over the howling wind and

the roaring water. "I'm gonna stay right here until I get the whole story."

Suddenly Sally laughed. Miss Carter and the X's and the numbers seemed far, far away. She was very happy here, with the wind blowing in her hair and Death around the corner.